ACF Bookens

BOOKS

By ACF Bookens

Vinci Books

vinci-books.com

Published by Vinci Books Ltd in 2025

1

A CIP catalogue record for this book is available from the British Library.
Paperback ISBN: 9781036704148

The EU GPSR authorised representative is Logos Europe, 9 rue Nicolas
Poussion, 17000 La Rochelle, France
contact@logoseurope.eu

Chapter One

For months, I had been studying the historic lay of the land by looking at the trees. I could spot, thanks to Dad's training, old homesteads by the presence of towering oaks, and I could tell where fence lines used to run by watching for the spires of cedar stretching across the fields. Sycamores told me where water was and where it had been in the recent past, and dogwoods signaled the edges of forests and farmyards that had once been. These signs had been easiest to spot in winter.

Now, though, I was torturing Sawyer on every car ride by pointing out the daffodil stems and iris fronds that were poking up along the side of the road. Clumps of the bright-green bulbs hung to the root balls of trees, and alongside the lane to our own farmhouse, I'd just spotted daffodils and crocus coming up in what would be a bright swath of color for us and for our neighbors.

My favorite batches of flowers, though, were the ones that came up where they seemed spontaneous. Along the edges of the road or in patches of pasture gone wild. These were the remnants of homes and families long gone. These were the bursts of sunshine they would have seen in the days when winter felt like it might never lift. I looked at these flowers – and urged Sawyer to, even when he literally growled at my suggestion – because these were the things that tied us to the people before.

And that was my work – pulling the pieces of history out of the past and setting them in the now. That's how I thought of architectural salvage, and, today, Sawyer and I were on the way to my newest salvage job at an old warehouse that had, in its final iteration after a hundred years of use, been a small printing house for letterpress books.

I'd gotten the lead about the building from a subscriber to my newsletter, where each month I told a story about a building or some aspect of history from our area and then talked about my salvage work. My subscriber list had been growing pretty steadily as people heard about what I did and realized I could talk about the places they loved and tell them stories they hadn't yet heard. Now, I was getting a few leads off every piece, and this warehouse was the most exciting so far.

The building wasn't sprawling like warehouses often are, which was good because I didn't have a big crew. What I did have, though, was my best friend's Uncle Saul, who had decided to become a silent partner in my business. He ran his own construction crew but as he climbed into his seventies had decided that doing the physical work wasn't really in his best interests. He had a great foreman, too, so when I had a new job to scout, Saul came along with me.

As Sawyer and I pulled up to the warehouse, I spotted the bumper of Saul's truck behind the building, and then I saw Saul with his suntanned and wrinkled face and his bright-yellow hard hat up in a third-story window. He gave a quick wave and a thumbs-up before he turned back into the building. I sighed with relief. His signal meant the building was sturdy and at least relatively safe, so Sawyer could come in with me. He would have enjoyed a movie in his car seat for a bit if necessary, but I didn't love doing that often. Plus, I really liked showing my son what his mother's work was. Not to mention that Sawyer loved scoping out any chance he could find to climb.

"Okay, Little Man, let's get your hard hat and go exploring," I said with a smile into the rearview mirror.

"I ready!" he said, and did the fist bump of excitement I'd taught him. "Let's go!"

Before getting out of the car, I poured a small bit of water into a travel bowl and set it on the floor of the passenger seat so that our cat, Beauregard, who had insisted on coming this morning, could drink. Beau didn't travel because of adventure. Beau traveled because he liked the heated seat. I didn't mind. He was fun to have along, especially when I had to give him a chance to do his business and walk him on his leash. A cat on a leash, it turns out, is a small but very real joy for many people who see him.

In the back seat, I unbuckled Sawyer, handed him his toddler-sized and very real hard hat, and held his hand as we made our way toward the warehouse. The building was two stories of brick, and it featured a central door that made it look a bit like the barns that were much more common than warehouses in this part of Virginia. The windows above the door were leaded glass, and most of them were still intact, a fact that I considered a miracle, given how bored teenagers are in the country.

As we stood on the small porch that served as a loading dock, I took a quick look at the land around us. It was mostly pasture, but I could see, just off the side of the building, an abandoned set of railway tracks that explained why the warehouse had been set here, seemingly in the middle of nowhere, at one point. I told my phone to remind me to look up the short-line railroads in this area.

Then, Sawyer and I went in, and I was immediately awestruck. The entire back of the space was made of windows – windows of all different sizes and styles that had been cobbled together to create a cascade of sunlight on the floor of the building.

I took a quick scan of the room, saw no gaping pits in the floor or open elevator shafts, and let go of Sawyer's hand so he could explore and I could get a look at this window wall. It was magnificent and reminded me of those recycled greenhouses that people made from recycled windows, only much more striking in its size.

"Pretty impressive, huh?" a voice said from across the room.

I turned and saw Saul smiling as he held Sawyer on his shoulders. "I'll say," I whispered as I touched my fingers to a nine-pane window. "We can salvage these, right? I might be able to sell them as a wall."

"Just what I was thinking," Saul said as he and Sawyer walked over. "Looks like they're attached with brackets of some sort. Should be easy enough to get down." He slid Sawyer off his shoulders, and my son barreled into me with the force of a waist-high bull.

"Awesome," I said as I took Sawyer's hand and moved around the room. I saw a few wooden boxes, and some of the beams overhead looked usable, as did the vintage light fixtures. But what I was really most interested in sat in a dark corner near the wooden stairs at the back of the building: three antique letterpress printing machines.

The owner had mentioned they'd be here and said that

while he knew they had some value, he just didn't have the time to sell them and hoped I'd be able to find them a good home. I had no doubt of that. The trick was going to be for me to part with them.

Each of the machines stood about shoulder-high, and while each one was distinct from the others, they all featured some components made from wood and some from iron. I'd done some research in preparation for this visit, so I was able to do a quick once-over of the machines to see if they were complete. From what I could see, they all had their ink plates and their rollers, but at least one needed new trucks—well, old trucks that would work like new ones. I felt confident I could get the parts they needed or find someone who specialized in the machines and would buy them because they could also get the parts.

As I ran my fingers over the ink plate of the largest machine, Sawyer said, "Look, Mommy, books," and ran over with a stack of saddle-stitched booklets.

I smiled. I could tell, just from the look of the covers with their purple-inked trillium and the titles "Poems for a Virginia Spring" that these were some of the books printed here in this building. I took the books from Saw before he could destroy them and flipped through one. It was full of beautiful illustrations of flowers, and each image was paired with a brief poem. I started to read one but was quickly distracted by the sound of little feet on wooden stairs.

Saul was right behind him, and I decided I didn't want to miss out on seeing what was upstairs. I tucked one copy of the book in the pocket of my grandfather's old shirt that I wore as a coat and slipped the rest back into a box before following Saul up the staircase into a surprisingly bright loft space. Clearly, this had been the main storage area for all of the businesses that had operated out of the building. I could see more books and also crates marked with the name of a local orchard that was still in business a ways up the road. In one corner, I found rolls and rolls of labels for tomatoes, and I wondered how many farmers had dropped their wagons full of produce at this building when it was a cannery. I made another note in my phone to look up whether tomatoes had been carried by rail.

I could feel myself getting excited. All of this stuff would sell – people loved vintage things that had ties to food – but more, I couldn't wait to research what businesses had operated in the warehouse over the years. That was going to make a great story for my newsletter.

Saul and I made another quick pass through the building and then stepped out back just to be sure there wasn't anything lying around that might be useful to Saul or sellable for me. In the past, we'd found stacks of T-posts for fencing that I'd been able to sell for two dollars a pop to a local farmer, and, at another house, Saul had pulled back a tarp to find four-inch-thick boards of Wormy Chestnut, a wood that was, for all intents and purposes, completely extinct. His excitement over finding the wood told me all I needed to know about how to thank him for all he'd done for me, and when I presented him with the wood, all cleaned up by Sawyer and me on a warm, sunny afternoon, he had choked up.

Now, that wood was going to be the flooring in a brand-new house that Saul's crew was constructing up on a mountainside. He'd even asked the owners if Sawyer and I could come see it as soon as it was in, and they'd graciously agreed and suggested we plan to bring something to leave our mark in the corner of the floor. Dad had loaned me his woodburning set, and Saw and I had written "Sutton" with a heart in the corner of what would be their living room.

Some historian someday was going to get very frustrated trying to figure out what Suttons had lived in that house, but the delight on Sawyer's face erased any guilt over putting my future colleagues to a futile task.

Today, though, all we saw was a stack of old pallets that I'd take for Dad and his primitive woodworking projects but that weren't worth much in cash, and a bunch of rubble piled over near the train tracks. Nothing much at all.

Still, this was going to be a lucrative job, and I was eager to get started, especially since I now had my very own staging and storage space over at Saul's construction head-quarters. He'd graciously offered me my own "boneyard" a couple of months back, and I was loving having a little workspace of my own. Dad and Lucille had even bought me a little shed to use as an office, and now I had a sign – hand-painted by my friend Mary Johnson – that said, "Pais-ley's Architectural Salvage" on the side of the building.

I wasn't yet Mark Bowe of *Barnwood Builders* fame, but I was getting there, one salvaged window at a time. To date, my most lucrative sale had been to a couple who bought all the beams we'd pulled from an old farmhouse. They'd recreated the basic footprint of that house for their living room and dining room and wanted to reuse the beams in as close to their original positions as they could. The finished product, which Saul's crew built, was a gorgeous post-and-beam-style house with large kitchen and master bedroom additions.

As I loaded Sawyer into his car seat after our walk-through, I asked Saul if his crew would like to take the lead on this demolition job or if I should hire another crew. I had been saving as much as I could to expand my business, and I thought I could afford to hire a crew for one day to get the main stuff. Then, I'd just hire a bulldozer and tear down the rest, per my agreement with the owner. He wanted the building razed and the rubble hauled away. That was another day or two's work, but since it didn't have to be done until July, I had time to save up again.

"Paisley-girl, you are not to be spending your money on a crew. That wood you gave me bought you rights to my crew anytime you need them for the rest of this year." He stared at me until I nodded. "And soon, you and I need to have a conversation about your next steps in the business."

I smiled over my shoulder and said, "Okay, Saul. Thank you." I was so very grateful for his help and so very uncomfortable taking it. But one thing I'd learned in the year or so since Sawyer's dad and I split was that I really had to accept help when it was offered.

"Help me with something now that Sawyer is secured?" Saul said. "It'll just take a minute."

"Sure, just let me get him some videos." I pulled the phone out of my pocket and handed Sawyer a bag of fruit snacks and his favorite videos of pandas that rescue people. "I'll be right back, Love Bug."

I closed the door and locked it behind me as I followed Saul back into the building. He led me down a set of stairs I hadn't even noticed and then used a crowbar that he took from his belt to pry open the slatted elevator doors.

There, stacked eight or ten high, were dozens of bags of potting soil. I had never understood why people bought soil this way when local farmers and soil-growers would bring it by the truckful, but apparently, the sway of the big-box stores held still, even way out here in the country.

"Spotted this earlier. I want to take it to that community garden those folks are starting where we took down that house up in the hollow a few months ago. You mind?" Saul bent to heft a bag onto his shoulder and onto a stainless-steel cart that reminded me of the ones they'd used to bring out the fixings for the salad bar in my college cafeteria.

I followed suit as I grunted out, "No, of course, I don't mind. Great idea. Thanks for thinking of it." I meant what I said, but, although I hauled thirty-plus pounds of toddler around most days, I was not finding it easy to heft a fifty-pound sack of wet dirt. The prospect of lifting fifteen or twenty more was not appealing.

Still, Saul and I got a few bags onto the cart, and then he wheeled it toward the rear of the building. Saul had propped the door there open with one bag of soil and I could see his pickup truck. It was probably twenty feet away, but it seemed like four hundred.

While I waited for Saul to come back with the cart, I started to use the strongest part of my body, my legs, to shift the bags from the next pile across the floor and closer to the door. I figured a few feet less to walk, even with a cart, was a win.

I was just beginning to shuffle the final bag in the front of the elevator shaft toward the back door when something caught my eye. I bent down and looked closely at the blue triangle I could see protruding from underneath the remaining bags. It was denim.

My heart started to pound, but I tried to take a deep breath and remind myself that many things were made from indigo-dyed fabric – purses, aprons, maybe some kind of bag that they used in this warehouse.

"Saul," I said in a shrill voice, "I think we need to look at something here."

He jogged over. "What is it? You didn't find another dead body, did you?" He jostled me with his elbow to accompany his not-so-funny joke. Then he looked at my face, and all the color left his.

I pointed down at the fabric on the floor and then began removing the bags on the left side of the elevator. Somehow, now, I had much more strength, and Saul didn't even huff as I handed him each bag to set beside us.

I was just reaching for the bag closest to the floor when he said, "Paisley, let me," and moved to step in front of me.

"No, I need to do this. It's my job, my business." I bent down and carefully shifted the bottom bag with my foot.

There, clad in bell-bottomed denim, were the bones of a human leg.

Given how long the body must have been there to become only bones, we knew there was no rush to move quickly. So by silent agreement, we worked carefully instead, shifting each bag away and revealing the body, a headband still hanging around the blondish hair dangling from the skull. The woman looked like she had just taken a seat to rest for a while, well, except for the fact that she was just a skeleton, that is.

Once she was clear and free, I stepped back and said, "Oh, Saul, not again."

Chapter Two

Sheriff Shifflett answered with a cheery, "Hello, Lovely," when I called, and I so wanted to have just called him to talk, to be simply in this first stage of dating where everything is new and rosy.

Instead, I said, "We found a body. I think it's a woman. She's been dead a long time."

I heard the hiss of air through his teeth before he said, "At the warehouse that you and Saul were scoping today?"

Santiago and I had sat on my porch the night before and talked about this project and the dreams I had for my business. Finding a skeleton had not been part of that dream. "Yes, in the basement, but I'm outside because Sawyer is in the car. Saul is staying with the body." I whispered the last word because my son was learning more and more vocabulary every day, and now, here he was with me for the third time when I found a body. I wondered if child protective services had a specific category for mothers who brought their children to crime scenes.

"I'll be there in ten." He paused.

"I know you have to say it. Go ahead."

"Don't touch anything."

"Got it," I said before disconnecting and calling my stepmother, Lucille. This was going to take a while, and I needed someone to come get Sawyer.

"I'm at the old warehouse off Lumbarton Road. Can you come get Sawyer?" I asked when she picked up her phone. "There's been another incident."

She didn't even pause. "Keys are in my hand. We'll be there right away. Maybe we could take Sawyer for lunch and then a little playground time before his nap?" Her voice sounded steady and sure, which was how my stepmother just was. The woman had been marching at war protests and fighting for civil rights in the sixties, and she was still a fierce warrior for justice. But she also baked the best breads and cakes, even trying her hand at chocolate croissants for me since I was still on a tight enough budget that I couldn't afford my favorite bakery treat very often.

"Good idea. I'll let him know you're coming. We're out front. Saul is in back, and Santiago will be here." I stepped a bit away from the car where Saw was, blessedly, still watching videos. "I'm going to tell him that Saul and I found something that the sheriff needed to see but nothing beyond that."

"Got it," she said. "See you soon."

Despite my disturbing penchant for finding bodies, I was not ready to talk with Sawyer about murder yet. I would not, unless absolutely necessary, lie to my son, but I also wasn't going to try to explain murder to a toddler.

It had to be murder. No one simply dies and then somehow hides themself in the bottom of an elevator shaft behind bags of potting soil.

That was the curious thing, though. From her clothes, I

would have guessed the woman died in the 1970s, more than forty years ago, but those bags of potting soil were pretty new. The bags weren't breaking down and faded. I'd seen that exact brand at the farm co-op the week before when I'd been picking up chicken food.

So, recently, someone had tucked that woman's body into hiding. I just couldn't figure out why. If it had been me, I would have moved the body out of the building altogether, buried her, maybe. I knew from the ache that was slowly growing in my lower back that most people wouldn't have been able to quickly and easily pile up those bags of soil like that. Goodness, it surely would have been easier to just – as crass as it sounds – toss her body over the bank behind the building and let nature cover her up.

I could feel the tightness that had formed in my chest when we found the woman growing big and threatening my breath, so I forced myself to think about other things, like those printing presses and the beautiful brickwork on the façade. I couldn't have a breakdown in front of Sawyer.

With an aplomb I'd seasoned over the almost three years of my son's life, I straightened my shoulders and walked back to him with a silly expression on my face. "Guess who's coming to get you?"

"Santa Claus!" he shouted.

I laughed. "No. Better. Baba and Boppy."

Sawyer tilted his head and squinted just a little. "Why?"

I sighed. "Because Mommy and Uncle Saul found something that Santiago needs to see, so I need to stay here for a little bit."

His frown threatened to turn into tears, so I quickly said, "BUT Baba said they're going to take you for lunch and then to a picnic at a playground. How does that sound?"

He smiled. "You come."

"How about this? I'll meet you there as soon as I can, okay?" I leaned over and kissed his round cheek. "Maybe you could get me a hamburger?"

His face got very serious, and he said, "I will do that, Mama." Then he paused and put up one chubby finger. "And I will get you a milkshake."

I grinned and sat down in the seat next to him to give him an awkward hug. I wasn't about to unstrap him until Lucille and Dad arrived. "Can I watch videos with you? Maybe some *BabyBus*?"

"Sure," he said and expertly clicked around to find his favorite video where the little pandas rescued other animals from a forest fire.

A few minutes later, Santiago's patrol car pulled in next to us, and Sawyer started squirming in his seat. He loved the sheriff, but he loved the sheriff's car more. "Can I play in Santi's car?"

"No, Love Bug. Remember, you aren't allowed to play in anyone's car but mine." I squeezed his hand. "Let me ask Santi to come see you though, okay?"

It was clearly a second-rate option, but it would have to do. I stood up and walked over to the man I was dating and said, "I'm so sorry."

"Did you murder this person?" he asked with a small smile.

"You know what I mean."

"I do, but, really, stop apologizing for being a good citizen." He squeezed my arm. "We are, however, going to have to talk about your knack for finding bodies."

I sighed. "Yeah. Have a minute to say hi to Sawyer?"

"Of course," he said, and he reached into his car, pulled out something, and walked over to Sawyer's open door.

"How are you, Sawyer?" he asked as he leaned into the

car. "Need a little something to play with in here?" He held out a paper airplane.

"An airplane," Sawyer said and grabbed at it.

Santiago pulled it back. "Be gentle, okay? It'll break. But you can fly it in here for a while, and then later, when you're outside, it'll go a long, long way."

My little guy tossed that little airplane in the air, and it flew right up onto the dashboard. His delight was contagious, and as Santiago headed behind the building, Sawyer and I turned the interior of the Subaru into an airfield.

A few moments later, he couldn't wait to show his grandparents his new toy, and as soon as I unstrapped him, he went zooming toward Lucille, airplane sound at top volume. She scooped him up and listened with delight as he explained how it worked.

Dad made his way over to me, and we strolled a bit toward the building. "Are you okay, Baby Girl?" he asked as he wrapped an arm tight around my shoulders.

I nodded. "I am. But gracious, that poor woman." I leaned into my daddy's shoulder for a minute. "Thanks for coming to get Sawyer."

Dad looked over his shoulder at his wife and grandson. "You know that we never mind extra Sawyer time. One of the perks of retirement." He winked at me. "Now, what do you think about that playground with the really tall climber? I'm considering that a perfect launchpad."

I laughed. "Agreed. You might need to fold a couple more airplanes, though? I don't think that one will be airworthy for much longer." We watched as Sawyer sailed the plane right into a puddle.

"I brought backups," Santiago said as he came around the building. "I'll grab them."

Dad reached out his hand and shook the sheriff's before Santiago headed to his car.

"He's a good sheriff," Dad said. "And a good man." He gave me one more squeeze and then moseyed back to the vehicles just in time to take an armful of paper airplanes from Santiago.

Lucille grabbed a reusable shopping bag from their trunk and quickly got the planes inside before they all ended up in the mud, too. "Time to go fly, Sawyer," she shouted.

I walked over, gave Sawyer a big hug, and said, "I'll see you at the playground soon."

"Okay, Mama. Bye-bye." He climbed up into his seat in Lucille's car and latched the chest belt all by himself, and I grinned. He was growing up, and while there was a sadness that came with that, I was also glad to see him getting more self-sufficient, for his sake as well as mine.

Dad got him buckled in the rest of the way, and I waved until they were out of sight. Then, I took a deep breath and followed Santiago back around the warehouse.

The coroner and Officer Winslow, one of Santiago's deputies, had arrived and come to the warehouse from a farm road next door. I was grateful for their discretion, even though I knew that it was as much about containing this story as it was about my son. I waved to Officer Winslow, and she gave me a small salute.

I stood a fair distance away from the back doors, my unfortunately growing experience with body retrieval telling me that they needed room to work. But I also knew I'd need to give a statement, either here or at the station, and so it was best if I stayed nearby, just in case.

The stretcher with the body bag rolled out the door, and I watched as the coroner and her assistant loaded their van and drove away. I said a silent prayer for the poor woman in that van, that her family could now find peace and with hope that she hadn't suffered.

I turned away to catch my breath and pull my tears back, and something moving in the woods caught my eye. It was Saul, walking slowly through the trees down below the warehouse. He must have needed some fresh air while he waited, too.

Officer Winslow waved me over, and I stepped inside the building after her. She and Santiago had set up bright lights inside the shadowy basement, and I was glad to get a better look at what was down there because I saw, across the room, a long machine with a belt that looked like it was part of an assembly line.

"Do you mind if I take a picture of that?" I asked the deputy as I pointed across the room. "When we can move things out of here, I might want to sell it."

"Feel free. Just be sure you face away from the elevator." She turned back to her careful movement through the area around where we'd found the body, and I walked across the room.

I felt a little callous, still thinking about my business, but if there was anything I'd learned from the previous two times I'd found bodies at my salvage jobs, it was that eventually I'd need to focus on making money again. It wouldn't serve anyone, even the victim, if Sawyer and I starved to honor some sense of respect that the victim wouldn't even be aware of.

Pictures taken, I wandered around the rest of the basement, trying to stay out of the way while also keeping my mind occupied. I didn't want idleness to send my anxiety up again. I was just about to turn the corner by the wooden stairwell we'd come down when I noticed a few boxes tucked under the stairs.

"Any harm in me pulling these out?" I shouted across the room.

Santiago stood, looked at what I was pointing toward, and said, "Just wear gloves." He gestured toward a white box of nitrile gloves by the door.

I walked over, slipped on a pair, and returned to the boxes. The first two were full of spare parts for one or the other of the machines in the building, so I took a picture to remember to grab those when we were able to load out. But the back box was chock-full of photographs, and I immediately carried the box over to Santiago.

"I don't know that these are important to your investigation, but I thought you'd want to see them." I held out the box, and Santiago nodded.

"Yeah, we'll need to take them back with us." He gestured to Officer Winslow, who took the box from me and wrote something on a slip of paper before sliding the entire box into a giant bag. "Maybe Paisley can help us organize the photos?" she asked the sheriff before carrying the box to her car.

"Now, that's a good idea," he said with one eyebrow raised in my direction. "Would you be willing?"

I thought for a moment and said, "I'm not a photography expert, but I'd be happy to take a look. Maybe tomorrow?"

"Sure. Mika could watch Sawyer at the shop?" Santiago knew my best friend was always willing to give my child the run of her store.

"I'll ask." I started to walk back toward the door so I could stand in the sunlight for a bit while I waited. "Actually, would you like me to ask Dad to come? He knows everyone in Octonia and has for his whole life. He might be able to identify some of the people in the pictures."

"Yes, please." Santiago nodded. "Great idea. I'll sit in, too, and maybe the three of us can make some sense of why those photos are in this building." He looked back toward the elevator shaft. "Maybe there'll be some clues about who this woman was."

I nodded. "If it's not too many people, Saul might like to help, too."

"Saul might like to help with what?" my gruff friend said as he stepped back into the basement.

"We found an old box of photos. Thought they might be important," Santiago said. "You have time tomorrow to help us look through them?"

Saul grimaced. "Sitting in a room and looking through a bunch of old pictures? Not really my favorite use of my time." He sighed. "But if it'll help. Just let me know when and where." Then, he looped his arm through mine and said, "Let me show you these naturalized daffodils out here."

I glanced over my shoulder to Santiago, and he was smiling. "We'll call when we need you. I think we can take your statements right here, save you a trip to town."

Saul nodded briskly and then led me down a deer trail into the woods. The very first buds were on the trees, and the maples were beginning to flower. I could even hear peepers singing at the edge of the stream to our north. Spring was definitely on her way.

"That was odd," Saul said, so quietly I almost didn't hear him.

"Well, for us, unfortunately, finding a body isn't really that odd." My attempt at humor was met with a sideways eye roll.

"No, I meant the way her body was tucked away like that. Why go to that trouble?"

I nodded as I stepped over a fallen tree. "I was thinking the same thing. If you wanted to hide a body, there are easier and more effective ways."

"Exactly." He stopped and studied a jack-in-the-pulpit peeking out from amongst the shade from the trees around. "I expect Santiago will have noticed the same thing."

"I'm sure he will, but I'll also mention it, make sure he understands exactly how we found her." I felt kind of bad that we'd moved all those bags, but at the time, it had seemed the right thing, a way to pay her some respect. Besides, if we hadn't, we wouldn't have found her remains.

Saul stood up and pulled out his flip phone. "If I knew how to get a photo off of here, it might help." He turned the phone to face me, and in the thumbnail-sized image, I could see the stack of potting soil.

"You took a picture? I didn't see you do that."

"You weren't down there yet. I snapped the pic and sent it to the garden owners to be sure they wanted to use it." He closed his phone. "It's the kind with fertilizer already in it, and I didn't know if they were going organic."

"Ah, I see." I put out my hand. "Let me see your phone."

He lowered his eyebrows but then handed over the phone. Within ten seconds, I had texted the photo to both me and Santiago.

"We better get back up there. The sheriff is going to want to take our statements, and that picture is going to give him a whole lot more questions, I expect." I slipped my arm back through Saul's and began to walk back up the hill.

It didn't take long for Santiago and Officer Winslow to get our statements, but that picture had raised some new queries. "She was completely surrounded by the bags? She was sitting up like this when you found her? There wasn't anything else in the square of bags when you began to move them?"

We answered all the questions, explaining that we couldn't see her when we began, that she was in exactly that position when we first saw her and that we took care not to move her, and that we hadn't found anything else at all with the body.

Officer Winslow and Santiago shot each other a long look, and then Winslow said, "Someone wanted her body to remain here. It was important."

"Just what I was thinking," the sheriff said as he closed his notebook.

"What does that mean?" I asked.

"The person who put her here cared about her or this place, probably both," Santiago said quietly.

"She was killed by someone she knew." Saul's voice was solemn.

This day had just gotten a whole lot darker.

Chapter Three

Lately, I'd been watching *Wynonna Earp*, a show Mika had turned me onto because she knew I'd love the tough women and the monster hunting. She was right . . . but now it was kind of playing with my brain about what might have been the reason that poor woman was left so intentionally in that warehouse. I was imagining rituals and portals that needed to stay closed and demons that rose again and again from the dead. The ride back into town to meet Sawyer, Lucille, and Dad was kind of freaky with all that supernatural speculation.

Fortunately, my call to Mika, who adored a good demon-chase on TV as much as I did, dispelled all that nonsense quickly. When I told her that we'd found a body and where it was located, she whispered, "Sounds like a lost love or something."

I paused and then said, "You know what? It does sound like that. Like someone wanted that person to remain with a place that was special to her, maybe a place important to the killer, or to the victim and the killer both."

"Like maybe they used to make out all the time there in high school, but as they got older, the victim decided she wanted to move on. The killer got angry, killed her, and then kept the body there to visit." Mika's voice was breathy with excitement at her theory.

I chuckled. "Slow down there, girl. I was thinking supernatural ritual myself. Let's not go all wild with the killer-revisiting-the-body stuff."

"Sorry. Too much *Dexter* for me, I guess. I went right to serial killer." Mika gave a nervous laugh. "Does Santiago know anything yet?"

"Nope, nothing." I sighed. "Not sure he'll tell me much when he knows either, which is okay because I do *not* want to make more work for him." Recently, Mika and I had tried to help Santiago, and it had almost gone horribly wrong.

"Good point," she said. "I've got to go, but still on for make-your-own pizza at your place tonight?"

"Yep. Sawyer is insisting that chocolate goes well on pizza."

"I love that. Dessert pizza for the win. See you tonight."

I smiled. I hadn't mentioned that Saw thought chocolate and pepperoni were the perfect combo.

Sawyer and I spent the afternoon wandering the fields around our house. He found about a million mud puddles, and I enjoyed watching his blond hair bounce in the sun and catching the arcs of bird flight as a way to keep from thinking about the skeleton in the elevator shaft. By the time we got back to the house as the sun was starting to set, we were both tired and calm from the exertion.

I gave Sawyer his videos on my phone and started to set out the pizza makings. The week before, Saw and I had made a few batches of homemade pizza dough, and this morning I'd set one out to thaw and proof. It was swollen and beautiful in the oven, and when I pulled it out, I punched it down and then divided it in two – one portion for our pepperoni and extra cheese main course and a smaller for our chocolate and peanut butter dessert course.

Then I set out sauce and other fixings before prepping my granny's homemade chocolate sauce. I was certain that Granny would have never considered chocolate on pizza, but given that most people never would have considered her chocolate syrup and biscuits a breakfast staple, I figured turnabout was fair play.

Just about the very moment I got everything ready, Mika pulled up. We'd started doing these Wednesday night dinners because it helped both of us out to split the cost of a meal, because it was fun to have our little family of choice together on a regular basis, and because I really needed some assistance with my rambunctious toddler at the end of the day. His dad spent a lot of weekend days with him, but these five-day stints without help were grinding.

Sawyer heard Mika's car pull up and went flying out the door in his bare feet. That boy could sprint across gravel and razor wire without a whimper. I, however, had to tiptoe if there were too many crumbs on the floor. I needed to learn some lessons in toughness from my son.

The making of the pizza was a free-for-all of flying cheese and chocolate-dripping madness, but eventually, we got two pizzas into the oven with a very minimal amount of chocolate sauce in with the pepperoni, much to Sawyer's disappointment.

"Take me on a tour of the daffodils?" Mika said to

Sawyer, who grabbed her hand and pulled her out the door. He loved giving tours of the farmhouse, and now that the plants were coming to life, he had expanded his tour to include various weeds and tall brambles at the edge of the yard.

"Come on, Beau," I said to the cat, who was quite upset that it had gotten too warm for me to turn on the gas fireplace. He looked at me out of one eye and then slinked off the couch as if it was his own idea. Soon, though, he was stalking a vole like it was his job – and of course, it was his job. I was just glad to see him doing it. He was actually a pretty stellar mouser when he felt like it.

I trailed behind Sawyer and Mika and listened to my son name the various trees – he knew maples and sycamores and cherries already – and he also pointed out where Beauregard had pooped recently. It really was a tour of the highlights.

After the sun had dipped completely behind the trees, we went back inside, and I deigned to light the fireplace for all of us, even though I let Beau believe it was just for him. And the three of us watched a few Morphle videos before I took Sawyer up to bed. It wasn't a completely easy lights-out because he needed several playings of "All Along the Watchtower" by "Bob and Dylan," but eventually, he wrapped an arm around my neck and went to sleep.

I slipped into my yoga pants and a huge T-shirt and then joined Mika on the couch. We had decided to try *Firefly Lane* together, so my binging of the Earp descendant's escapades was going to have to wait. We weren't far into the first episode, though, when my mind started to wander.

I kept thinking about the skeleton, about what the victim was wearing, about how she looked like she'd walked right out of a disco with her bell-bottom jeans and the sparkly headband. If we had lived in a place where dance clubs were an actual thing, I might have not been so bothered by the clothes, but the nearest club was in Charlottesville. Maybe someone had brought the body to Octonia to hide it.

"Earth to Paisley," Mika said. She had paused the show and was waving a hand in front of my face. "Where'd you go?"

I smiled and shook my head just a little. "Sorry. I was thinking about the body. Did I tell you what she was wearing?"

"No, you didn't." She put down the remote. "Tell me."

I described the jeans and the denim jacket. The macrame shirt and the headband. "I mean, it was classic seventies. Almost too spot on."

Mika folded her legs under her. "Halloween?" she asked.

I considered that. "Maybe. Or maybe a themed dance or something?"

"Hold on." She grabbed her phone out from under her leg and began typing frantically with her thumbs.

I had never mastered that skill. I had to hold the phone in one hand and type with my pointer finger. At least I knew the keyboard, though. Dad was still hunting and pecking two decades into the twenty-first century. He was so slow that I wanted to rip the keyboard out of his hands anytime he went to type.

"Here it is." She handed me the phone. "I knew I saw something like this recently."

On the screen was a flyer for a dance to be held the next week at the local VFW hall. "Can You Dig It?" was written in a huge yellow font across the top of the page, and below it were the details of a seventies-themed dance to benefit a local food pantry. But what really caught my eye were two phrases: "costumes requested" and "twenty-third annual."

"Whoa, so maybe she was at this first dance?"

Mika nodded vigorously. "Maybe. Worth telling Santiago about, right?"

"Definitely. Mind if I text this to him?"

"Please." Mika picked the remote back up. "I presume we need to start back at the beginning."

I grinned and winked. "If you don't mind."

"I don't mind at all. I get to watch Brandon Jay McLaren all over again." She grinned and pressed play as I sent my text.

Beyond a quick emoji reply to Santiago's note of thanks, I ignored my phone and let myself get sucked into the drama of television. The fact that it was about the lifelong friendship of two women felt so fitting, given that I was sitting with my best friend of more than two decades. By the end of the first episode, we had both cried, grabbed each other's hands, and laughed loudly enough that I worried we might wake Sawyer. I wasn't sure the show was that incredible, but this woman beside me was.

The next morning at her shop, Mika and I exchanged a warm look as I handed her a super-huge double espresso latte from the coffee shop across the street. We'd had some wine with our TV drama binge, and while we both were responsible drinkers, especially with Sawyer in the house, the dehydration headaches were a real thing.

"Bless you," she said and immediately took a huge swig.

I hissed, worried that she'd just taken all the taste buds off her tongue. The barista of the morning had said he was brewing things extra hot to help take off the frosty chill of this early spring morning, but Mika wasn't fazed. I would have developed blisters. I'd had to take the lid off my own mug and blow on it all the way across the road just to get mine cool enough that I could sip it.

Sawyer had wanted his usual chocolate milk, and I was very glad I'd thought to put it into one of his lidded cups because he was already on a tear through the store with Mika close behind. "Saw, let's get out the playdough. I have an idea," I could hear her saying as she steered him toward a small table in the back.

I laughed and sat down in one of the wingback chairs in the center of the store. Recently, Mika and her employee, Mrs. Stephenson, had created a fairly private and totally cozy little work and conversation space with a few armchairs and some carefully placed bins of yarn. Now, customers – or people who wanted to talk without the prying eyes from the street – could sit and knit, peruse patterns, or whatever, without feeling like they were on display. Mika still kept two more armchairs by the front window, and often people chose those because they liked to people watch when they sewed or because the natural light was better for their eyes. But when anyone wanted privacy, The Cozy Nook was the choice.

Now, I pulled a small trunk away from the wall and situated the three soft chairs around it before grabbing a fourth folding chair from the back. Then, I brought out the box of coffee I'd gotten when I grabbed our lattes and put out a stack of paper plates. Lucille was going to send some baked good, I knew it, so I wanted to be prepared. Next, I put two paper bowls, one with creamers and one with sugar packets, on the trunk. Only then did I realize that we were not going to have any room to look at photos with all this stuff out. I also realized that the three men who were about to arrive were going to razz me about that.

I girded my loins for the teasing and sat back to enjoy my latte while I waited for them. From the checkout counter, I heard Sawyer say, "Look, Auntie Mickey, I made a 'pider web."

Just then, the chime on the door rang, and Mrs. Stephenson came in, looking rosy and sweet. The woman was an accomplished business owner, and I knew from the way she handled would-be shoplifters in here that she was a force. But today, especially, she looked like Mrs. Claus, and I kind of just wanted her to hug me.

She gave me a little wave and headed right for Sawyer. I heard his feet pound toward her, and I knew that he had just hugged her legs. Then he said, "Mrs. Steffason, did you bring me a surprise?" and I groaned. We were going to have to have a talk about that later.

The door chimed again, and Dad and Saul came in, looking as thick as thieves. They'd known each other since first grade, and, for years, they'd had breakfast together every Saturday morning. This morning, they'd revisited that tradition with sausage biscuits out at the Gas-N-Go outside town. I knew because I'd offered to pick up Dad on the way in.

Unfortunately, it did not look like they had brought me a sausage biscuit, but on the upside, Dad did have one of Lucille's plastic containers in one hand. He smiled, raised it shoulder-high, and then set it carefully in the center of the trunk. I didn't even pretend to want to make small talk, and if I had, my stomach would have growled too loudly for me to be heard. "What did she make today?"

"No idea. She said to let you open it." I smiled and then realized, somewhere in the back of my mind, that I was behaving just like Sawyer and wondering what Lucille's surprise for me was. I was going to have to have a good talk with myself later, too.

When I lifted the lid, the smell triggered another stomach growl, and I lunged for a sausage roll like I hadn't eaten in days. These were one of my favorite things that Lucille made.

The smell must have reached Dad, too, because he groaned. "She made those to spite me," he said. "She was miffed that I didn't invite her to come along. That must be why she stayed up so late last night."

I sighed at the thought that my stepmother had my back. "Well, next time, you can invite me for sausage biscuits. Or better yet, we can ask Lucille to cater for us and both get much better food than you can get at the gas station." The Gas-N-Go biscuits were actually really good, as was their fried chicken, but nothing compared to Lucille's sausage rolls.

Dad and Saul took the matching wingbacks and helped themselves to coffee just as Santiago came in. I tried to maneuver my way from behind the trunk so that I could sit in the folding chair, but he was quicker than I was and plopped down before I could get there. Not that I was complaining. I had a giant latte, a super comfy club chair, sausage rolls, and no means to get out and mind my wild and rambunctious son. But I did want to make an effort to be courteous.

Then, as if on cue, Saul said, "Now, how exactly are we supposed to look at photos if we have a four-course meal laid out on our workspace?" He looked at me and huffed before winking.

"Actually, let's sip our coffee a minute while I give you a bit more information." Santiago's voice had taken on the authoritative tone that he only used in the most serious situations. "Paisley and Mika sent me a photo last night that gave us a key piece of information about the victim. It seems the victim might have been at one of those seventies-themed dances the VFW has every year."

"They're still doing those?" Saul said.

Dad nodded. "It's weird, isn't it? That they do the same decade every year. Why not change it up?"

"The costumes. Those VFW guys don't want to buy new costumes," Saul said.

That made a lot of sense. "You think she'd been at the dance?"

"We do. The clothes were made more recently than the seventies – at least that's what our initial internet searches indicate – so we're not looking at a decades-old murder here." He ran his hand over his chin. "But we'll know more after the coroner finishes her autopsy."

I studied him for a minute. "There's something more you need to tell us." He looked like a man who just couldn't quite get the words out.

He sighed. "Yeah. So the clothes the skeleton had on were women's clothing, definitely. The sizing, the styles – definitely made for a woman." He cleared his throat and cut his eyes to Dad and Saul. "But the skeleton was male."

I sat back. That was a plot twist. "Someone in drag?" I said, thinking of all the parties I'd been to in my life where people used drag as a party trick or joke.

Santiago shook his head. "No, this person also had on, um, undergarments that indicate they were pretty serious about changing the appearance of their anatomical features."

Dad leaned forward and said, "So she was trans."

I stared at my dad. Not only had he known what

Santiago was saying, but he had used the right pronoun. I wanted to hug him.

———————

We spent a few minutes discussing whether this victim's gender identity could have been motive for killing her, and we all knew it could have been, especially here in a place where change comes hard. But as Santiago cautioned us, just because it could have happened didn't mean that it did happen. "We have to wait for evidence," he said.

I nodded and began to clear up the paper plates and coffee supplies so that we could use the trunk to look at the box of photos that Santiago had brought out of the evidence closet at his office. He handed around blue nitrile gloves, and we all put them on. Then, I lifted out the first stack of pictures.

I wasn't a photography expert, but I'd shuffled through enough boxes of photos from old buildings to begin to understand how to tell how old they were. For example, those with scalloped edges are mid-twentieth century, and of course, most people my age know Polaroids from our 1970s childhoods. And those beautiful silvery ones printed on plates of glass are daguerreotypes from the middle of the nineteenth century. I'd read up some on tintypes and cartes de visite, but I didn't know much about those types of photographs yet. Fortunately, though, most of these looked like twentieth-century images.

We began by sorting them into piles by size, style, and shape. Deckled edges went in one pile. Color photos in another. Polaroids another. Santiago had brought along a stack of numbered stickers, and as we sorted, we gave each image a number.

We had a stack of vintage postcards, too. Most of them were blank, but a few were written on and could, maybe, give us more information about who had been in this warehouse when. Maybe. Of course, it was also possible that this person had a penchant for old images and had just gathered them up from yard sales and flea markets. But I was hoping that wasn't the case.

Once the photos were sorted, we started a round-robin with each of us looking at each photo and identifying folks. Santiago and I knew some people because we'd both grown up here, but we were no match for Dad and Saul, especially when it came to the older photos. Soon, they were spouting off names and stories faster than I could make notes. I gave Santiago a wide-eyed stare and said, "I'm getting Mika's help."

Sawyer was contentedly talking Mrs. Stephenson's ear off by the register, and there were no customers in sight. So I tugged Mika bodily away from her restocking task and said, "I need your help."

"Right," she said. "You could just say that rather than trying to detach my arm."

I dropped her hand. "Sorry. It's just, well, this is a lot."

She patted my shoulder. "I know. What do you need?"

"Help me take notes on what Dad and Saul are telling us?" I handed her a piece of paper and a pen.

"Seriously?!" She grabbed another folding chair, sat down, picked up her phone, and said, "Ready?" Herein was a fundamental difference between my friend and me – digital versus analog.

Santiago smiled and said, "Thank you," before picking up his own pencil – a pencil! – and continuing to take notes on what he saw in the photos while Mika and I captured what Dad and Saul said. The numbers Santiago had brought were invaluable because we could simply start with number sixty-seven, say, and then record anything we noted.

After a half hour or so, I noticed a pattern. "Have any of you see any photos of families? Or pictures taken in people's homes?"

Saul stopped mid-sentence in his story about the local baseball field and showing films against the backdrop after games. "No, I haven't, now that you mention it."

"Me neither," Dad added. "So these are all photos from public events?"

Santiago nodded. "Good catch, Paisley. Yeah, that seems to be the case."

Mika put down her phone and poured herself a cup of coffee from the box on the floor. "Who would have a collection of public photos?"

"A newspaper," Mrs. Stephenson's voice came like a clarion call from over the bins behind me.

I stood up and almost knocked over the dregs of the latte at my feet. "Of course. This must be from the *Ledger*." The *Octonia Ledger* had been in print since 1877 when the county was founded, and while it was quintessentially small-town with its coverage of local fairs and police reports that typically focused on fake 911 calls, it had always been and still was the center for all local news in the area.

I picked up the box the photos had been in and studied it. Sure enough, there on the top flap in handwriting that was almost invisible under dust, I read the words "Ledger Photo Archive" out loud.

Mika guffawed. "Some archive. The folks at the Special Collections Library would be losing their minds." She wasn't wrong. The archivists I knew were stringent about keeping their holdings safe and secure, as they should be.

"I expect these were discards, just backup images not considered very important." I studied a few of the photos with the newspaper in mind and realized that while the images did show people, they weren't ideal because some had blurred faces or turned backs. "I wonder if the newspaper kept the ones they actually used."

"Want me to ask the editor? She's a friend," Saul offered.

Santiago shook his head. "Thanks, Saul, but I'd rather a reporter not know about this stuff until we have more to share, if you know what I mean."

Saul stood and stretched. "Completely. No articles until you can control the story. Got it." As he sat back down, he asked, "Do you have time to go through the newspapers to find out what stories go with these?" He looked weary and wary about even asking the question.

"No, I don't think we do. That could take hours and hours," the sheriff's said solemnly. "I wonder, though, could we ask Ms. Nicholas?"

"At the historical society?" I grinned. "She would love this project, and we could give her what information we've recorded here. Between that and her own deep knowledge of Octonia, I bet she'd be able to whip through these and get us the relevant stories."

Mika put up a hand and said, "I know we can trust her, but just want to ask one question – what do we think we're going to find in the photos? Are we trying to identify our victim? Or find out who might have killed her?"

Santiago said, "I think at this point we're just trying to figure out anything related to our victim and who might have been using the warehouse about the time she was killed."

"When will the coroner let you know when she died?" I asked.

"This afternoon at the latest, I expect." He looked at his watch and stood. "I should get back to the station, but, Paisley, I've signed this box out to your care. You'll talk with Ms. Nicholas and let me know?"

"Headed there right now," I said as I stood and put on one of my grandfather's old flannel shirts. "Need me to write up anything if I leave the box with her?"

"Just email me with an update. That'll suffice." He turned to Dad and Saul. "Gentlemen? Thank you."

Dad shook Santiago's hand. "Always fun to take a walk down memory lane, especially if it helps someone."

"Any idea when we'll be able to get back to work at the warehouse?" Saul asked and then winced. "Don't mean to sound callous, of course."

"Nope, I totally get it. We all have to pay our bills," Santiago said with a glance at me. "Winslow and I are headed out there soon to take one more look around. We'll probably keep the elevator shaft sealed, but I expect by tomorrow you all can get back to salvaging. I'll let you know."

I followed him to the door. "I'll let you know what Ms. Nicholas says."

"Please do." He leaned over and kissed my cheek. "Up for a porch date tonight?"

"Nine p.m. it is." I watched him walk up the street before turning back to see three pairs of eyes on me.

"He's a good one, Paisley-girl," Dad said.

I nodded and hurriedly returned to our trunk to repack the box of photos. I wasn't really interested in talking with my dad about my love life.

Chapter Four

Xzanthia Nicholas was one of my favorite people in Octonia, and not just because she loved me. She was a no-nonsense woman whose kindness ran as deep and strong as her backbone. When I walked into the historical society offices that were just up the street from Mika's shop, she greeted me warmly with a hug and then a stern, "You have not been here enough, Ms. Historian. We need each other."

I blushed. She was right. I'd been so busy with parenting and my business that I'd not done a lot of the history work I needed to do, the work I loved to do. "I'm sorry," I said as I hugged her again and breathed in the warm scent of the coconut oil she used on her chestnut skin. "You're right. Today, though, I have some big-time history for us to do if you have a few minutes."

Ms. Nicholas did her usual joke of looking around the empty historic house and saying, "It seems I may have some time." And then she grabbed the box from my hand and said, "Ooh, photos!"

We sat down at the long table in the research room, and she said, "Now, tell me the story of these."

"Well, first, I know you wouldn't talk about what we discuss—"

"Say no more, my dear. All work done here is kept in the strictest confidence. No one needs to know your family's secrets but you." She winked. "So are these *your* family secrets?"

I smiled. "Not that I know of." Then, I told her about the woman in the warehouse and how the box of photos looked to be the discards from the *Ledger*. "We're hoping you can help us identify which stories from the *Ledger* these photos might correspond to."

Ms. Nicholas took out a stack of photos and nodded. "You've sorted them roughly by decade, I see. That will help." She turned a couple of photos over. "And you've numbered them. Also smart."

"Dad and Saul went through some of them, and we made notes on who they recognized and from where." I held up my handwritten notes. "I'll type these up and get you Mika's and Santiago's too if that would be helpful."

She continued to sort through the pictures. "Most definitely would. Most definitely would."

I could see she was already disappearing into the stories these photos told. I'd worked with her many times, and the things Ms. Nicholas knew about Octonia could fill volumes and volumes of books. "What do you think? Is this a project you have time for, well, now?" I cleared my throat. "Time is of the essence, of course."

"Yes, my dear. To help this poor soul find peace, I will put aside all other matters." She looked up at me then. "May I bring in one assistant? With two of us, we could sort the photos and then compare them to the newspaper archives at a much faster clip."

I thought for a second and then decided, as I knew Santiago would, that if Ms. Nicholas thought someone trustworthy, we would too. "Yes, please do. But of course—"

She patted my hand as she said, "I will make sure they understand the sensitive nature of this project."

I squeezed her fingers. "Thank you. And if I have more information I can share about the victim, I will." I stood and looked over her shoulder as she gently but assuredly began to further divide the photos into stacks.

"These are related to the holiday bazaar. These seem to be the high school." She was talking to herself, as I did, as she made sense of the information before her. "I will let you know as we begin to make progress," she said in a clearer voice with a quick glance in my direction.

As I looked back from the front door of the museum house, I could see her still talking through her thoughts as she moved one picture after another into the right pile. She was going to have this done in no time.

As I walked back to Mika's shop, I texted her: *You guys okay for a few more minutes?*

Totally. Do what you need to do?

Okay, I'm headed to the sheriff's office. Be back in twenty.

Take your time.

The day was beautiful, and while I knew better than to wish for it to be a little warmer, given how quickly a Virginia summer can arrive, I was looking forward to those scant few days of spring where I could go without a jacket entirely and feel the sun on my arms. Today, though, the air was just a bit too brisk for that, so I settled for feeling it on my face as I walked the few blocks further past Mika's store to see Santiago.

He was sitting at the front desk taking his rotation to greet guests and answer calls. The department was small, only two full-time officers, and while they often had a dispatcher and a receptionist, Santiago also believed it important that he do any task his subordinates did. Plus, as he told me when I arrived, it was good for people to see his face front and center. "Lets them know I'm paying attention and am informed."

I smiled. I liked that mindset, a lot, especially since many of the sheriffs from my childhood had been focused on intimidating people into compliance instead of connecting with and serving their constituents.

I sat down at the chair next to the desk and told him Ms. Nicholas was on the job. "I told her only the barest minimum because I wasn't sure what you'd feel comfortable with me sharing."

He smiled and then took my hand. "I appreciate you thinking of that. Let's tell her that our victim was a twenty-eight-year-old white trans woman. The coroner thinks she was probably a natural brunette, but her hair had been bleached."

I nodded. "Okay, I'll let her know. That should help her be able to spot the victim in photographs." I put both my hands around his. "This is hard, I know. You doing okay?"

"I am. But an unidentified victim is taxing because it's hard to investigate and because . . ." He didn't finish his sentence.

"Because you can't notify the family until you identify the victim?"

"Yeah," he said. "It's a weight to carry the prospect of delivering that news around for so long."

I couldn't imagine. I'd done one notification, and it had been so painful to witness that mother's grief. "Well, if I can do anything else to help . . ."

"I will let you know."

I stood and gave him a quick hug. "I'll see you tonight."

He nodded and leaned over to answer the phone as he waved.

I stopped by Mika's for a quick update and to pick up Sawyer. He and I decided today was the day for a treat, so we swung through the local drive-through and got two hamburgers, fries, and two milkshakes. Saw made it through two bites of burger and most of his fries before sleep caught up with him.

I decided to use the quiet time to think and enjoy the blooms of spring, so I drove around looking for quince bushes on the back roads. I wasn't intending to go back to the warehouse, but my thoughts were so clearly tied to the place now that I wasn't actually surprised when it came into view over a low rise in the road.

Saul's truck was in the lot, and he and an older Black man were talking as they leaned against the hood. I pulled in and quietly shut my car door. "Hi, Saul. I see you got drawn back here, too," I said with a smile.

"Actually, I came intentionally. Paisley, this is Robard Greene." He looked over at the other man. "He used to work here."

"Oh, Mr. Greene, it's so nice to meet you," I said as I shook his hand. "What a beautiful building to work in."

"It's more beautiful to me now," he said in a booming bass voice. "Then, I just wanted to get away from the smell of tomatoes so quickly that I barely looked at the place." He smiled.

"Oh, so you worked here when it was a cannery?" I thought of the machine in the basement and wished I could show it to him and get him to explain how it worked.

"Yes, ma'am. It was my first job. I was in charge of loading the crates into the boiler." He rubbed his neck as he spoke.

"Oomph, that sounds like hard work. And hot, too." I grimaced. I didn't mind physical labor, but in the Virginia heat, no thank you. Just weeding my garden beds was going to be enough for me come July, and I was going to do it first thing in the day, even then.

"It was so hot." He turned back to Saul. "But you asked me to come out for a reason."

Saul turned his blue eyes to me and said, "I talked with Santiago, Paisley. We're clear."

I took a deep breath. I was glad Saul had run this conversation idea past the sheriff, and I listened quietly as Saul told him about how we discovered the body in the basement and what the coroner had said about her age and appearance.

As Robard listened, his face grew grimmer and grimmer. When Saul had told him everything he could, Robard took a long, slow breath and said, "I think that may be Celeste. She used to work for me." He swung his fist and banged hard enough to leave a dent on Saul's truck, which would have been a gross violation of friendship under any other circumstances. Now, though, Saul barely gave the divot a glance.

"Anything else you could tell us about her that might confirm her identity?" Saul asked quietly.

Robard studied his friend's face for a minute and then said, "She had the body of a man."

A small moan escaped my lips, and when Robard looked at me, I said, "We can't be sure, of course, but it does sound like this is Celeste."

Saul nodded and put a hand on Robard's shoulder.

Robard leaned back against the truck. "She was more than an employee. She was like a daughter to me. Anytime she needed anything, she knew she could come to me, and I would help her. She didn't have an easy life" – he looked from me to Saul – "as you can imagine."

I glanced back to be sure that Sawyer was still asleep and then said, "The sheriff could really use your help with this, I think." I remember how haggard Santiago had looked the night before as he talked about identifying Celeste's body. "He wants to make a positive ID as soon as possible so he can give Celeste's family some closure."

Robard's eyes flashed as he stood straight up. "Those people deserve no closure. They cast her out, forced her to live in a shed until she broke free. They do not deserve to have closure." He was practically shaking with rage.

I took a step back and looked to Saul for help.

Saul nodded slowly. "Okay. So let's see what we can do about helping find her killer, okay?"

Robard gave a crisp nod and then looked toward the building again. "She loved this place, called it her Sanctuary, even asked one time if she could put a little apartment in the basement." His eyes scanned the building. "I would have let her, too, if the building codes had allowed it." He grew quiet.

I had a million questions to ask, but I knew it wasn't my

place. Santiago would need to get everything on record, and I had learned my lesson about getting too involved in a case. Still, for my own curiosity about the building, I had to ask one thing. "You own this building?"

Robard smiled. "I do, Ms. Sutton. I had hoped to keep my workings with you anonymous just so that you could feel comfortable taking anything you wanted from the building. But given the circumstances . . ."

I turned toward the building. "Did Celeste work for you at the cannery?"

This made Robard laugh, and it was a glorious sound. Big and full and rumbly. "No, ma'am. Celeste was my book-binder. A great one, too." He stared off in the middle distance. "I closed the cannery down as soon as I bought the building. Overhead was too high with shipping and production to pay my employees well in that business. Instead, we became an elite letterpress publisher. Had clients in New York and San Francisco, and it was a business that allowed all of us to make a good living while also producing beautiful things."

I suddenly remembered the small booklet I had grabbed and patted my hands against my pockets to find it. When I pulled it out, Robard smiled. "I found this inside, a whole box of copies, in fact." I handed it over.

"She did it," he said. "She never told me." He opened the book and read a poem before closing the book again. "Can I keep this?"

I looked over at Saul who nodded and said, "I don't see why not. We'll let the sheriff know you have it, but it was in another part of the warehouse from— Who wrote it?"

The smile that broke across Robard's face was brilliant. "Celeste did. She was quite the poet, and she'd always wanted to produce her own book. I told her she could use our equipment anytime, but I just assumed she hadn't gotten around to it before she disappeared." He held the little purple book up again. "But she did. I never even looked at what was inside when I shut down production a year or so after Celeste went missing. I just couldn't keep it going without her, and I didn't really want to."

My throat was tight, and I felt like I might cry. Instead, I said, "I really do look forward to learning more about your friend. She sounds amazing."

Robard cleared his throat. "She really was." He slid a straw hat with a red ribbon onto his head. "Now, I best be getting down the sheriff's office. Saul, I could use the company."

"You've got it, old friend," Saul said. "Talk to you later, Paisley."

I nodded and leaned against my own car hood as the two men got into Saul's truck and drove away. As I studied the beautiful brick building, I thought of Celeste and really *really* hoped that Santiago could figure out what happened to her.

I was just about to get back into the car to begin our drive home when my phone rang. It was Xzanthia. "Hi, Ms. Nicholas. Everything okay?"

"More than okay, Paisley. Can you stop by this afternoon? Bring Sawyer if you need to. It'll only take a minute. I want to introduce you to someone."

"Thirty minutes okay?" I asked.

"Sure thing."

"Great. Sawyer will just be waking up, so if you have chocolate milk on hand, it might buy us a few minutes."

"I will have the needed sustenance," she said. "See you soon."

45

Sawyer was still snoozing soundly when I got to the historical society. I took out my phone and replied to a few emails until he began to stir. I hefted my boy out of the car and held him close while I walked around to the front of the historical society. As I began to climb the stairs, he looked at me and then around us and said, "Good morning."

"Good morning, Love Bug." I pulled him closer and kissed his cheek. After a couple of minutes of snuggles, I said, "Saw, we're going to see Ms. Nicholas. She has choco-late milk."

He smiled and said, "Okay," and put his head back on my shoulder. He was getting heavy, but at this point, I was just hoping I wasn't carrying him when he went to his first day of kindergarten.

Ms. Nicholas was waiting inside, and she'd set up a small area with a set of crayons and paper and a small lidded cup full of Sawyer's magical elixir. I got Saw settled in and then joined her at the nearby worktable, where our photos were clearly ordered into some sort of system.

"We're well on our way, Paisley," she said and began showing me how she'd organized each photo by decade and then by event. There were piles for the high school home-comings and proms, for the county fair each summer, and even for some big church gatherings, as those were often the social events most people attended.

One pile caught my eye when I read the label: "VFW dances." "This one. We were wondering if—" I paused before I said Celeste's name. Santiago needed to have that information and decide how to release it. "If our victim might have been attending one of these dances, given how she was dressed."

"That's exactly what we were thinking," someone behind me said.

I turned to look, and a young man with the most amazing pink mohawk I'd ever seen sat down across from me. He looked like he'd stepped right off the set of one of those reality shows where people are way cooler than me. The hot-pink stud in his left nostril looked amazing against his dark skin, and I really wanted to know where he'd gotten that awesome topaz ring on his pointer finger. The fact that he was clearly about my age made him look all the more amazing. I loved when middle-aged people kept an adventurous personal style. But I held off on getting fashion tips until I could hear what he had to say.

"Paisley, this is Trevor LaMon. Trevor, Paisley Sutton." She smiled at me and said, "Trevor is my nephew, and he's studying for his master's in history at UVa. I thought he might be able to get some firsthand experience and help out with this project."

I smiled and reached across the table. "Nice to meet you, Trevor. Glad you can help." I looked back at the stack of photos. "Tell me about the dance, if you don't mind?"

He nodded and set down the stack of files he was holding. "Looks like the dances started quite a while ago." He flipped open a folder. "And they held one last summer, so we're looking at almost twenty-five years of dances."

"Whoa, okay. I saw the flier for the twenty-third one. A quarter-century of bell bottoms and disco is a lot." I smiled at Trevor, who grinned back at me.

"Yes, sister," he said. "So many afros to tend." He patted his mohawk. "So if we find out what year our victim died, we can probably figure out whether she was at this dance."

I nodded. "Okay, I think the coroner will have that information soon. I'll let you know when I know." I paused and looked at the two kind people at the table with me, and then I glanced over at Sawyer, who had moved from coloring to watching his videos and seemed quite content. "I also need to give you a bit more information about our victim. She was twenty-eight years old, white, and transgender."

Trevor sat back hard in his chair. "Whoa."

Ms. Nicholas frowned. "How do you know? I mean, I don't want to be rude, but you said she was just a skeleton."

I sighed. "What she was wearing. She had padded certain areas, and there was some tape." I really didn't know enough about how trans people managed their anatomies to speak formally about this stuff, so I stopped there.

"I'll explain more later, Auntie, when young ears aren't nearby," Trevor said with a nod toward my son.

I smiled. "But that may matter, you know, so as you look through—"

"Of course that matters, most of all because we're looking for a young, blonde white woman." Ms. Nicholas gave me a pointed stare. "The other matters only if it, well, matters." She clicked her tongue and went back to a notepad in front of her.

I swallowed. "Exactly," I said, and hoped against hope that Celeste's gender identity didn't matter here at all, except in the way that central things about our lives matter to each of us. "I really hope that her identity isn't what got her killed," I said.

Trevor was staring out the window beyond Sawyer, and he looked worried.

"Me too, my dear," Ms. Nicholas said.

"Yeah," Trevor said as he pulled his eyes back to us. He was still frowning, but he also looked eager to work. "I'll start pulling the articles about these events."

Part of me really wanted to stay and help them research, but I had a little boy who needed some outside time. Sawyer and I said our goodbyes and headed home, where he played outside for a few hours, and I prepped our garden beds for our first round of seeds. By the time dinner rolled around, I was as enthusiastic about the usual nuggets and noodles as Sawyer was.

After dinner, we read a few books and played with his trucks, and then, he dropped off like the cliff of sleep had opened before him. If Santiago hadn't been coming over, I might have just stayed in bed and slept a full twelve hours with my boy.

Instead, I got up, pulled a new scarf into my hair, and prepped a new blend of tea my friend Jamila had whipped up. It was all rose hips and rosemary, delicious and fragrant. Some men might have disliked the scent, but I knew Santiago. He didn't abide by those stereotypes of what was masculine or feminine.

Right at nine, Santiago knocked quietly, and I opened the door with a smile. He stepped in and gave me a soft kiss first thing. I had trouble forming words after but, fortunately, I was able to carry mugs and walk toward the front door. Santiago followed, and soon we were in our chairs with our lap blankets and mugs, looking at the thousands of stars in the sky. Sometimes I missed the convenience of living in a town, but mostly, I adored the twinkling stars and the song of the peepers.

"Thanks for sending Mr. Greene down to talk to me. We will have to wait for dental records to confirm, but it sounds like our victim is indeed Celeste Davenport."

I had thought he would be happy to have a probable ID, but instead, he looked upset. "That's not good news? I mean, at least you can inform the family."

He looked up at me quickly, as if he had been somewhere else in his mind, and said, "Yeah, that's the thing. I know her family, and they aren't going to be easy to talk to about this."

"What do you mean?" I had a feeling I was about to get very, very angry.

"You know the Davenports in town? The ones who own the assisted living facility behind the library?"

I nodded. "Only by name. Well . . . and reputation." I sighed. "Not my favorite people, I admit." When Mika had bought the building where she opened her shop, the Davenports had tried to enforce all kinds of antiquated restrictions about her apartment above her yarn shop, saying it was "a code violation" for her to live there. The county board of supervisors had disagreed, as had the other business owners on the street, and ultimately the Davenports had been forced to back down. But they'd continued to bad-mouth Mika, intimating that she was running an "untoward" business in the apartment. Mika and I had tried to laugh at the idea of her running a brothel when she couldn't even find a man she wanted to have dinner with, but we'd both been really, really angry.

"Yep, Celeste was their child." Santiago pushed the heels of his hands into his eyes. "I have to go tell them tomorrow."

I groaned. I could not imagine what people who thought a woman living alone in an apartment on Main Street might say about their trans daughter, but I knew it wouldn't be good. "You do? I mean, Celeste was a grown woman. Maybe you don't have to tell them at all. I mean – she was a grown-up." I cringed at my use of the phrases I shared with Sawyer.

Santiago smiled at me. "I don't, really. But can you

imagine the trouble they'd cause if I didn't?" He let out another long sigh. "I'm just struggling with how. I've been reading all day about how to talk to and about trans people with respect, and using their birth name is never part of the conversation. And yet . . ."

"And yet, if you don't, they may deny that Celeste was their daughter." I let my head fall back against the chair. "Here's the thing. Their denial is their problem, right? I say do the notification using Celeste's real name and leave it at that."

He reached over and squeezed my hand. "You're right. I'm overthinking this. Her name was Celeste. That's all that matters to me as far as my job is concerned." He took a deep breath and said, "Okay, so let's talk about something fun. What new swear word is Sawyer trying on now?"

I laughed. My son had heard his father and me say a couple of choice words at moments of frustration and had been experimenting with our reactions. Fortunately, we'd managed to mostly ignore the language after an initial explanation that those are words that we don't use often and never in certain situations, but he was bound and determined to find something to rile us up.

"This week, he's trying out *shoot* because that's what I say most of the time when I forget something." I smiled. "He's very emphatic."

Santiago smiled. "I bet. Have you introduced him to *good gracious* yet?"

"I have not," I said, "but he does whip out an *oh my goodness* from time to time."

"Now, I'm going to have to ask for that, next time we hang out." He took a sip of his tea and sat back. "Any word from the historical society yet?"

"Oh yes, right. They did find something, but first, let me

ask if it's okay with you if I tell them Celeste's name?" I looked over at him. "After you do the notification, of course."

He nodded. "Yep, once the Davenports know, I expect word will spread like tiny-town wildfire, so feel free. In fact, I'm thinking of asking the paper to run an article in Thursday's paper that gives the actual facts of the case to try and control the rumors."

"And her parents' disacknowledgment of who she was?"

"That, too. This poor woman was already murdered and hidden in a profoundly strange way. The least I can do is try to help her legacy be about who she really was." He finished the last of his tea and stood. "But now, I think we both need some sleep."

I stood and stepped toward him. "Yes, but first, I need this." I leaned over and kissed him gently.

Chapter Five

The next morning, just as Sawyer shoved an entire piece of bacon in his mouth, I got a text from Santiago.

Celeste Davenport – born August 23, 1987. Died in 2015. Dental records were a match to the ones her parents submitted when she "disappeared."

It's good you have an ID but also, ugh.

That about says it. Also, Robard Greene filed the original missing persons report in February 2015. It took her parents three months to give the sheriff any information.

I'm trying not to swear.

Me, too. I'll let you know how the Davenports take it.

Please do. Good luck.

As I ate my piece of bacon, I studied my chubby-cheeked son. I tried to imagine anything he could do, or anything he could tell me about who he was that would make me lock him in a shed or banish him from my presence. I literally couldn't think of anything, nothing at all, and I certainly wouldn't do that if it turned out he was actually a girl. That child was my beloved, and nothing would ever make me love him less or treat him as though I did. I could not understand the Davenports.

But I did understand hate, had seen enough of that in my lifetime to know that it distorted everything. I said a silent prayer for Santiago because he needed all the support he could get, and then I packed Sawyer into his jacket and headed to his swing set out back.

For the next hour, I tried to focus on the way he wanted to show me all his moves on the firefighter's pole at the end of the monkey bars, and when I just couldn't do that anymore, I faked my enthusiasm while I loaded my garden cart with sticks to put at the edge of the yard for our "wild-edge" fence.

Fortunately, Saw was ready for some juice and some videos when Santiago texted and asked if I could talk. I got Sawyer set up on the couch and stepped into the pantry, where I could hear my son but hoped he couldn't hear me.

"How did it go?" I asked when Santiago answered.

"About as well as we could have hoped." He groaned. "They were not happy when I called her Celeste, and I just ignored them when they used her birth name. It was a battle of wills, but given that I was on the side of goodness and love, I think I won."

"I'm sure you did," I said. "Did they give you any information that was helpful?"

"Not really. They kept wanting to know when they could bury 'their son,' and I stalled because I'm trying to figure out a work-around that keeps them from violating her like that."

It was my turn to groan. "They get to make those kinds of decisions after locking her up?"

Santiago sighed. "Well, the 'shed' of rumors wasn't quite what I expected. It was a really nice pool house, and they insisted Celeste was allowed to come and go as she pleased. But to answer your question, yes, they are still her parents and thus her legal next of kin, so they decide."

My stomach ached. "Would it be inappropriate for Mika and me to organize a memorial for Celeste? I mean we didn't know her, but maybe we could find people who did. And quickly, before her parents can harm her even after death." I had no idea how I could pull a service off, but I was bound and determined to figure it out.

"I think that would be lovely, and I'm sure Robard Greene would help." Santiago moved the phone away from his mouth and said something I couldn't hear. When he came back, he said, "Sorry, Pais, I have to go. Keep me posted?"

"Yep," I said just before he hung up.

I didn't even set the phone down before I called Saul. Sawyer was happily occupied still, and I didn't want to wait to enlist help on the memorial.

Saul listened as I explained what we now knew about Celeste's death and how Santiago had a positive ID. But when I began to explain how her parents were planning to move forward with a burial under her birth name, he cut me off. "I know them, Paisley. They're reprobates. You don't need to say any more."

I sighed. It made me sadder and sadder each time I thought about how these parents couldn't honor their own child's identity, so I was glad to be spared having to put that sadness into words. "Okay good. I want to honor her with a memorial of our own. If you can text me Robard's number, I'll call him and ask if he'll help."

"Yes, do that. We'll remember her well. I've got food and drinks covered." For a second, I thought he'd hung up, but then he said, "Thank you, Paisley. Let me know what Robard says?"

"Sure thing." I peeked around the corner and noted that Sawyer had moved on to playing with his trucks. I had another five minutes tops.

I dialed the texted number, and Mr. Greene picked up on the first ring. "Paisley Sutton, to what do I owe this honor?"

I paused a minute, surprised he'd known it was me.

"Saul gave me your number, and caller ID is a magical thing," he said.

I smiled, although I still felt a little uneasy, and not just because I had to explain to him about the Davenports. I tried to be succinct. "The Davenports want to bury Celeste as a man and use her birth name."

Robard hissed. "I figured they would want to do that, so I'm glad they don't have the legal right."

I cleared my throat. "Excuse me, did you say they don't have the legal right? They're her parents. What do you mean?"

"Years ago, Celeste appointed a friend as her legal next of kin. She knew her parents wouldn't respect her wishes and her identity, so she did all she could to protect herself." He sighed. "It's not a sure thing. Her parents will most definitely protest, but it at least means that if we can move fast enough, we can have her buried and a stone made with her actual name."

My heart was beating quickly at the hope we might be able to do right by this woman. "It takes forever to get a stone carved, though, and does she have a burial plot?" I didn't want anything to derail this one small thing we could do for this poor woman, but this one small thing required a lot of other smaller things.

"Trevor LaMon will know all the details. I'll call him and make a call to a friend who owns a gravestone company. We can move fast."

I started to thank him, but then my brain caught up with my emotions. "Did you say Trevor LaMon?" I remembered the charming man with the nose ring from the historical society.

"Sure did. You know him?"

"Um, yeah, just met him." I cleared my throat. "I'll see him a bit later today and can follow up then if you want." I needed a minute to think about why Trevor hadn't mentioned Celeste earlier.

"Sounds good. I'll give him the heads-up and tell him to look for you later."

"Thanks. I'll give you a call tomorrow to talk details?"

"I'll look forward to it and be in touch before then if need be." Robard hung up, and I sat down just in time for Sawyer to come charging toward me. I pulled him close and smelled his sweet head. A lot of people cared about Celeste, and maybe their care made them cautious. But I couldn't shake my memory of the look on Trevor's face when I told him about Celeste. I really hoped he didn't have something to hide.

I decided I wanted to see what Ms. Nicholas and Trevor were finding – at least I tried to pretend that's what I was doing. What I really wanted to do was figure out why Trevor hadn't told me about his connection to Celeste. So I texted Lucille to see if Sawyer could come over for a playdate.

She replied quickly: *Actually, I was hoping to come spend some time at your place, soak up some sun. Be there in thirty minutes?*

Perfect. I'll have lunch for us all.

I put the phone in my lap and said, "Baba is on her way to spend the afternoon with you. Do you want her to drive you for your nap or sleep on the couch?"

My son, never one to be confined to the choices offered him, said, "Nap in my playground."

Lucille could handle anything, so I said, "Sure. Should we take a blanket and pillow down there for later?"

He grabbed the pillow off the couch and ran and tumbled with it down the hill to his two-story tower. I handed up the blanket I had carried down behind him, and to my surprise, he put the pillow down, covered up, and stayed there. I took a seat in a chair nearby and expected him to pop up thirty seconds later. Instead, I finished an entire Instagram post about an old chimney Sawyer and I had explored a couple of weeks earlier, responded to all my Facebook messages, and checked my email. When I stood up, he was sound asleep.

After shifting him so that he couldn't possibly roll off the platform, I walked back up the hill, opened all the windows at the back of the farmhouse, and set out a lunch of cold cuts, cheese, chips, and the sun tea I'd hurriedly put out on the platform in the garden. When Lucille arrived, we took our seats on the front porch, in easy hearing range of the playground, and feasted to the delight of birdsong. It was beautiful and relaxing, and I was glad to get the chance to talk to my stepmother without interruption, a rare gift.

We sat on my porch in the warm spring sun and basked in the warmth, faces up to the sunshine and pant legs rolled up as we ate salami and cheese and listened for Sawyer. Eventually, though, I sat up and said, "Okay, so I could use your opinion on something."

She turned her head in my direction. "I'm all ears."

I caught her up on everything I'd learned about Celeste today and then told her about Trevor. "Why wouldn't he tell me he knew our victim?"

Lucille opened her eyes. "Did he know he knew your victim?"

I stared at her. "A trans woman's body is found in Octonia . . . How likely is it that it's not his friend who went missing a few years ago?"

She sat up and met my gaze. Then, she just held it.

I started to squirm. I didn't like this. "What?!" I finally blurted.

"Paisley, are you saying that Celeste is the only trans woman in Octonia?" She kept staring.

I sputtered. "No, I mean, of course not, but—"

She didn't let me finish. "And are you saying that Trevor had some sort of obligation to reveal his relationship with Celeste to you because he is doing this job?"

I sat back and stared at my hands as I mumbled, "No, I guess not."

Lucille sat back and put her face to the sun again. "What are you saying?"

The insight of Lucille's questions left me speechless for a moment, and then I said, "I guess I need to talk with him, to hear what he has to say."

Lucille smiled and patted around on the arm of my chair until she found my hand. "I think it's very likely that this young man did suspect that this was his friend, but if someone you loved had died, wouldn't you hope against hope that you were wrong, that you were jumping to conclusions?"

I sighed. "Of course."

"And while you and I know you are trustworthy, this young man may not know that. I expect his friend suffered a great deal of discrimination because of who she was. Maybe he has for being her friend. You need to earn people's trust, Paisley, not expect it to be given." She gave my hand a squeeze and then stretched out again as she slid a piece of turkey into her mouth.

I adopted a similar pose as the insight of Lucille's kind lecture sank in. She was right. I had been presumptuous to assume that Trevor would trust me, and I had jumped to conclusions about what Trevor should have known and told me. I needed to get my head straight before I went and talked to him.

Fortunately, a little nap in the sun did just the trick.

———————

A few minutes later, catnap complete, toddler still asleep and safe in the shade of the tower, and Baba settled into a chair nearby, I headed downtown with Beauregard. He had insisted on coming, perhaps because he realized our house was about to get particularly wild with Baba in charge. She had a far higher tolerance for Sawyer's physical antics than I did, and it was a beautiful thing to see them toss and tussle all around while they played. Well, I found it beautiful. Beau did not.

He sat and looked out the window as we drove, and a couple of times when birds danced at his eye level, he did that delightful chatter that I chose to interpret as "hello, Birdy Friends. It's good to see you," instead of "come closer, and I will eat you," which I suspect was more accurate.

Still, he was entertaining, and there is something soothing about driving quiet roads with your hand on the back of a furry friend. As we drove along, I thought about how to talk with Trevor about his relationship to Celeste. I most certainly did not want to be intrusive or rude, but I did think it important he know the situation with the Davenports and that he talk to the sheriff right away. I hoped I wouldn't even have to suggest that, honestly, but I would if necessary.

More, though, I didn't want to seem like I was taking over something by planning this memorial. It felt awkward now that I knew someone who, presumably, Celeste had really trusted. Maybe I could hand the event off to him, but even that idea felt wrong because it wasn't fair to expect someone to take something on that was my idea.

I was kind of a mess about all of this, and so when I saw Ms. Nicholas and Trevor having tea on the front porch of the society museum, I decided to do what I'd long ago learned was best when I didn't know what to do: listen.

"Hi," I said tentatively as I stepped out. "May I come up?"

Ms. Nicholas waved and stood. "Please. We were just talking about you, in fact." She pulled another wicker chair from the grouping at the other end of the porch and gestured toward it when I climbed the stairs. "We've mostly concluded with your research project and have located articles or announcements related to most of the photos."

I smiled and said "thank you" to both of them, but when I looked at Trevor, I paused. His eyes were red-rimmed, and he seemed washed-out, very tired. I started to ask if he was okay, but I quelled my passive-aggressive tendency to use platitudes of care to get information and simply smiled and waited.

"But we have, we think, a pressing question for you." Ms. Nicholas put her hand on Trevor's arm. "Have they identified the young woman whose body you found?" She looked intently at Trevor as she asked, and he gave a slight nod.

I took a deep breath and said, "We have. Celeste Davenport." I paused as Trevor took a shaky breath, then said, "Robard Greene tells me you knew her."

He nodded. "I did. She was my cousin and my best friend." His voice broke, and as he began to cry again, I took his other hand in mine and let him have his time.

After a few moments, he looked up at me and said, "I suspected it was Celeste when you first told us the victim was trans and that she may have been at a dance. Celeste loved to dance." He smiled a little. "She didn't care if anyone danced with her. Her body just moved to music and made her feel alive, she always said."

"Did you find a picture of her at a dance?" I asked. "I'd really like to see what she looked like."

Trevor reached into the pocket of the suit vest he was wearing over a Def Leppard T-shirt and handed me a small photo. In it, a gorgeous white woman with platinum blonde hair had one hip jutted out to the side as she lifted her pointer finger in the air, John Travolta–style. She was smiling, and her face was alight with joy. "She is beautiful," I said as I handed the photo back to him. "And I can see what you mean about how she loved dancing, even in that photo."

He nodded. "But that's what may have gotten her killed." He dropped his face in his hands.

Ms. Nicholas picked up the thread of his words. "We

are thinking someone may not have liked that Celeste was trans and at a dance as herself."

I sighed and squeezed Trevor's hand. "I see. Did she feel like she was in danger? Did she ever tell you anything like that?" These were questions the sheriff would need to ask as part of his investigation, but now, I just wanted to help Trevor and hoped that allowing him to talk would be helpful.

"No." He shook his head and looked up at me. "She never said anything. But here" – he waved his hand around at the collection of old houses surrounding the historical society building – "it wasn't just her parents who wouldn't accept who she was."

He didn't need to say more. I loved my hometown, and I loved rural life. But I also knew that isolation sometimes meant prejudice rooted more deeply. "I'm sure the sheriff is looking into every angle." I sighed. "He'd really like to talk to you."

Trevor looked at Ms. Nicholas and then back at me. "I'll go see him this afternoon."

"Good." I looked intently at Trevor and said, "He understands. And he wants justice for Celeste. He really does." Then, despite the fact that I knew it would be painful for Trevor to hear, I told him about the Davenports' intention to have their daughter buried under her birth name in their family plot at the town cemetery.

His eyes flashed. "They can't do that. I'm her next of kin, legally. She made sure of that. Years ago. What can I do?"

I felt a flush of hope, even as I could see the panic in Trevor's eyes. "I'm not sure, but talking to the sheriff is a good start. And maybe we need to get an attorney involved." I watched Trevor's face fold for the third time.

"I can't afford an attorney." His voice shook.

"Let me worry about that. And I had an idea, something that might slow the Davenports down a little. What if we held a memorial for Celeste in the next day or two? Invited the newspaper, got the word out on social media?" I waited while Trevor's face shifted from sadness to what looked like joy.

"I love that idea," he said. "I'll organize it if you'll help." He looked at me.

"Of course, I'll help." I smiled and felt my nervousness about this situation fade away and get replaced by determination.

"You can hold it here," Ms. Nicholas said. "I'll get the board's approval immediately, but given Trevor's work here, I can't see it being a problem." She stood up. "I'll make sure it isn't a problem." She stomped into the house.

I turned to Trevor. "Well, that's sorted," I said.

"Absolutely. No one crosses Ms. N," he said with a grin. "Is tomorrow too soon?"

I shook my head. "The sooner the better, I think. The Davenports will likely try to move quickly, so we just need to be faster."

He slid a pen and paper across the table to himself and began to make a list. "Do you know the editor at the paper?"

Ms. Nicholas came back out. "I know the editor. What do you need?"

"We want her to run a story. Do you think she will?" Trevor asked.

"I have no doubt. We'll get the details worked out. And the board approves and fully supports this idea. The building is yours. When are we doing this?"

"Tomorrow, if that works," Trevor said.

"Perfect. I'll see if the editor can write up something to go online today and then get into the Saturday edition tomorrow morning." She turned to go back inside. "You have the rest of this handled?" she said as more a statement than a question.

Trevor nodded, and she turned on a heel and went inside.

"If you handle the memorial and publicity, I'll take care of the food and drinks. My friend Saul offered, and I think we can pull together a fitting spread for your friend, maybe at my friend Mika's shop?"

"That would be great," he said with a smile.

I patted his hand as I stood. "Robard Greene is working on getting her a tombstone quickly, and let me get on that lawyer thing if you'd like. I have an idea."

Trevor stood, stepped around the table, and hugged me. "Thank you," he whispered in my ear. "Thank you."

I stepped back and looked at him. "I am honored to help. You will owe me two things, though, when we're done." I smiled.

"Anything. What do you need?"

"First, I need to know what that cologne is because you smell incredible."

He laughed. "I make it myself. I'll get you some. And the second thing?"

"Come to my house for dinner with me and my son some night? I'd like both of us to hear more about Celeste." One of my goals as Sawyer's mom was to help him understand that every person is beloved, and the easiest way to do that was to help him love as many people with as many different backgrounds as possible.

"Deal. I'm vegan, though," he said.

"Not a problem. I make a killer veggie stir-fry, and I can

cook tofu with the best of them." I laughed and turned toward the steps. "Oh, wait. I need your number."

He took my phone, entered his contact info, and then sat back down to his list.

As I walked down the steps and turned toward town, I smiled. This was going to happen . . . but when I saw the patrol car in front of the station, my heart sank. Celeste's murderer was still out there, and they weren't going to like all this publicity.

Chapter Six

I started the walk to Mika's shop to let her know that I'd volunteered it for the reception after the memorial. I knew she wouldn't mind, mostly because she cared about Celeste, too, but also because foot traffic in her store was good for business.

But first, I needed to take care of finding a lawyer for Trevor, and I knew just who to call. Saul answered immediately, and he knew just the person to recommend. "I'll take care of the cost, too," he said. "Tell Trevor not to worry."

"Thank you, Saul," I said before giving him Trevor's number and telling him about the memorial the next day.

"I'll be there, and I'll ask some of the guys to come, too. Just in case the Davenports make a scene." He hung up before I could thank him again.

The idea of there being a scene at a memorial service made my stomach plummet again, so I stopped outside of Mika's store and called Santiago. I told him about the plans for the memorial service and about Trevor's concerns about why Celeste died.

He listened and said, "He just called me, and I'm meeting him at the coffee shop in ten minutes. Thanks for suggesting he get in touch."

"Of course. I'll be at Mika's for a while if you want to stop over."

"See you later, then," he said, and I could almost hear the smile in his voice.

Mika was busy with a customer, so I took a seat in the front of the store while I waited. I had emails to check, and I didn't mind a few minutes of peace to just bask in the sun some more.

My quiet time was short-lived, though, because a young blond man came in the shop and looked a bit lost. Plenty of men knitted and crocheted, of course, but the fact that he couldn't have been more than thirty-five, was dressed in khaki pants with a crease so sharp I could have cut carrots with it, and had a haircut that cost more than most of my wardrobe made me think he might not be there for yarn.

"Can I help you?" I said as I set my phone aside and stood. "Are you looking for someone?"

He turned to me and said, "Yes, Paisley Sutton. Is she here?"

I tilted my head. "That's me. How can I help?"

"I'm Kyle Davenport." He put out his hand to shake mine.

I hesitated. I really didn't even want to touch a Davenport after what I'd heard about them this morning, but my manners overcame my disgust as I extended my hand. "Nice to meet you, Mr. Davenport. What can I do for you?"

"I just saw this," he said as he held up his phone for me to see. "I came right over to see how I could help."

I looked at his screen, and there was a huge image that said, "Remember Celeste!" along with details about the memorial service time and the reception to follow here. Trevor had listed me and him as organizers. I was touched.

And also now very nervous. "You want to help with Celeste's memorial?"

"Yes, yes, I do. Very much. She was my sister, my big sister, and I really want to honor her well." He pointed to a chair. "Do you mind if I sit down?"

"Please," I said and sat opposite him. "You said you want to help?" I asked again as I tried to keep the incredulity out of my voice.

"My parents have made no secret of what they thought of who my sister was, and this morning, I heard them tell the sheriff that they'll be burying her" – he literally shuddered – "under her birth name. I'm not going to let that happen if I can stop it."

His story sounded credible, and I wasn't about to deny a brother a chance to honor his sister. I nodded. "Okay then. We would love your help. Let me text Trevor, and see if it's okay to give him your number."

Kyle shook his head violently. "No, Trevor isn't going to want my help. Please don't contact him. I saw the post when a mutual friend shared it, but he and I aren't connected anymore." Kyle tugged on his chin. "I didn't use to think this way about my sister. I was awful. She and Trevor cut me out of their lives."

I sighed. "To protect her? From you?" This situation was getting more and more painful and more and more complicated.

"Right. They were right to do it." Kyle paused to clear his throat. "I just wish I could apologize to Celeste . . ." He looked up at the ceiling and swallowed hard.

"Well, we can definitely use help here, but I will need to give Trevor a heads-up, of course. I don't want him to be surprised when you're here." I wondered how Trevor would take that information and just hoped he'd understand.

"Of course, and I'll give him plenty of space, even at the memorial. I just really need to help somehow." His cheeks were flushed, and his enthusiasm so intense that I felt some of my lingering misgiving slide away.

The bell on the door chimed, and Santiago came in. "Perfect timing. Santiago, this is Kyle Davenport. He's here to see if he can help with the memorial service. Kyle, this is Sheriff Shifflett."

Santiago stood very still and studied the young man. "Kyle, I was actually going to ask you to come to the station. I have some questions you need to answer. If you're free now, we can head on over."

I stared at Santiago and then over at Kyle, who looked even more dumbstruck than I was. "Santiago, Kyle was here to help—"

"I heard you, Paisley." His voice was sharp, but there was a plea in his eyes. "But right now, I need to have a conversation with Mr. Davenport. After you," he said as he pointed at the door.

Kyle looked at me, and I thought he might cry. "Sheriff Shifflett is a good man, Kyle. Just answer his questions truthfully, and then call me. We'll get you involved in the memorial." I scribbled my number on a piece of paper and handed it to him. "Don't worry."

After they left, I dropped into a chair and tried to process what had just happened. Mika joined me and handed me a cup of peppermint tea with lots of milk and honey. It was just the balm I needed.

"What's going on?" she said as she sipped from her own mug.

"That was Celeste Davenport's brother, and Santiago just took him in for questioning," I said flatly.

"He arrested him?" she asked.

"Not quite, but it didn't feel like Kyle had much choice but to go." I sighed. "He was here to offer his help for the memorial tomorrow."

"Oh, there's going to be a memorial for Celeste tomorrow? Where?"

I groaned. "Well, at the historical society but then here . . . I came down to tell you that I'd volunteered your shop, but then I got distracted." I opened my phone and showed her the announcement that had quickly spread through a lot of folks in Octonia. "It's kind of a done deal. I'm sorry. I should have asked."

Mika laughed. "No problem, but yeah, maybe next time ask. We're doing food and things, I suppose?"

"Actually, Saul is supplying everything, and I thought I'd ask Lucille to bring something if she has time." I suddenly felt very overwhelmed with the whole thing and put my head in my hands. "This is important, but how am I going to do this?"

"You aren't. *We* are. Call Lucille, and I'll do a quick inventory of our stash of paper products. We may need your dad to do a Costco run." She stood up and headed to the back of the store.

Lucille and Sawyer were taking a walk, but she offered to make a few dozen cookies and a special cake to honor Celeste. She also offered for Dad to get the rest of the supplies we'd need. I thanked her, told her I'd be home soon, and got Mika's list of what we needed. We decided we should plan for a couple of hundred folks to account for the lookie-loos who might just come to see what all the fuss was about.

By the time we had our preliminaries squared away, I was emotionally and mentally tuckered out and eager to just spend some time playing with my boy. When I pulled into the driveway, he came running. "Let me show you what I can do, Mama," he said.

Lucille and I trailed him back down to his playground to see his new feat of hanging from his knees and his hands upside down from the monkey bars, with two pairs of hands below him. "Wow, Love Bug. That's impressive." I almost said something about how he'd soon be able to use his legs to move across the bars but thought better of it just in time because I didn't think my heart could take it when he tried that out.

I gave Lucille a big thank-you hug, and she headed out to bake. I sat down by the playground and watched my son climb. He seemed quite content, since his grandmother had lavished him with attention, to play on his own as long as I was nearby, and I was grateful. I had some thinking to do, but first, I needed to be sure Santiago was still coming by tonight. I had a lot of questions, and I needed a little reassurance, too. That whole encounter with Kyle had left me feeling nervous about the situation with the sheriff and me.

Me: *You still coming by at nine?*

He replied immediately: *Of course, and I'm sorry about earlier. I'll explain. But that was some kind of awkward.*

It was, and whatever you can tell me, I'd appreciate.

Absolutely. I'll bring wine.

Sounds good. See you later.

Can't wait.

I was a forty-six-year-old woman, and still that kind of simple sweetness set my heart all a-skipping.

Before I could set my phone down, it rang. It was Kyle Davenport. "Hi, Kyle. Everything okay?"

"I think so," he said. "Maybe. I don't know." His voice was tight and stilted. "I answered the sheriff's questions as honestly as I could. But I still think I'm a suspect."

I sighed. "I'm not going to lie. You probably are, but not any more than anyone who knew Celeste, I'm guessing."

"Yeah." He paused. "Anyway, I still want to help with things for tomorrow. What can I do?"

I wasn't sure what the situation was with Kyle, and I didn't want to stir up any problems with Santiago or for Trevor. But something told me this young man just needed a role, some way to honor his sister. "Can you come to Mika's shop before the memorial to help us set up?"

"Absolutely. What time?"

I suggested noon, which would give us an hour before the service, and he thanked me and said he'd be there.

My strategy was to have Trevor at the historical society setting up at the same time, and hopefully, we could avoid any confrontations.

My phone rang again, and this time it was Ms. Nicholas checking to be sure Mika was comfortable with the arrangements and saying that all was going well on their end. She finished telling me that part of her reason for calling, but then she paused. "Paisley, I feel like I need to tell you something just so you are prepared."

I sighed. I was feeling a little bit overwhelmed by the number of confidences I was keeping at the moment, but I said okay and pulled my knees up to my chest to listen.

"Trevor's past is a bit, um, turbulent," she said. "He got in trouble for breaking into some abandoned buildings years back, just acting out, but it did give him a record."

"Okay," I said. "We all make poor choices from time to time." I meant that, but a bit of agitation was also tickling at the back of my brain.

"Yes, we do. I knew you'd understand that." She paused again. "But there's more. He also had some pretty serious run-ins with the Davenports, specifically Mr. Davenport."

"Celeste's father?"

"Yes. Trevor was the one, you see, who helped Celeste leave her parents' house. He got her out, but Mr. Davenport caught him. Tried to press charges against Trevor for kidnapping." Ms. Nicholas's voice was very small.

I sighed. "But Celeste was over eighteen, so that wasn't possible?"

"Exactly," she said. "But when Mr. Davenport couldn't find Celeste, he spent a lot of time making things very miserable for Trevor." She cleared her throat again. "He basically made it impossible for Trevor to find work in Octonia."

I let my head drop back against my chair. These Davenport people were really something. "Okay. So we need to keep an eye on things tomorrow." I took a deep breath. "There's something else. Kyle Davenport came to see me today."

"Is that so?" Ms. Nicholas said, and I could almost picture her arching one eyebrow.

"I wasn't sure what to do, so I suggested he help Mika set up for the reception. He told me that he and Trevor didn't get along, and he didn't want to cause Trevor any trouble."

"Mm-hmm," Ms. Nicholas said.

"But he seemed sincere, and if he's very sorry for the way he mistreated Celeste and Trevor . . ."

Ms. Nicholas sighed. "You did the right thing, Paisley. But we do need to prepare Trevor. I will talk to him."

"Yes, we do need to prepare him, but I can call him,

explain. I want him to know I was really trying to do the right thing." I felt like crying. This was all such a mess.

"Let me talk to him first. Then, tomorrow, when he's had a chance to prepare, you can be sure he understands your intention." Her voice was firm, and I appreciated that, as much as I wanted to call Trevor right now, she knew him better. She got to make the call.

"Okay," I said. "I'll come a little early to help set up and talk to him then."

"An excellent plan, Paisley." She spoke firmly once again. "And Paisley, you are doing a good thing. Good things, though, are often hard things."

I smiled. My life experience had taught me that, but I often forgot it. It still seemed like *kindness* should mean *ease*. "Thank you," I said.

As I put my phone down, I switched it to silent. Anyone else who wanted to talk to me would need to leave a message. I needed some time, and I needed to swing with my son.

After Sawyer was in bed, I picked up my latest cross-stitch project, a picture of a black-and-white cat in a sewing room. I'd bought it maybe fifteen years ago when I was house-sitting for a friend and found myself with lots of downtime. It had reminded me of my mom, and I had made a lot of progress over that week. But then, it had gone into the hatbox that holds my projects and laid unfinished all this time.

Now, I was back to work and loving the vibrant colors and whimsical layout. The image did remind me so very much of Mom's sewing room. She'd wasted no time converting my old bedroom into her craft room the weekend after I moved out of the house after college. She had stacks of fabric arranged by color for her quilting projects and bins and bags of yarn for her crochet. Her embroidery floss was no longer used for cross-stitch, but she kept some on hand for hand-stitching on art quilts. Now, her floss was mingled with mine in storage bins inside her old sewing cabinet.

This project, however, came with all its own floss, and I spent almost as much time figuring out which color I was supposed to be using as I did putting the needle to fabric. Still, I began to relax as I took up a vibrant royal blue and began to stitch in the curtains behind the head of the cat.

I turned on *Making It!*, that charming craft show with Amy Pohler and Nick Offerman, and let myself disappear into the simple world of hand-making things. Soon, I was onto my second episode and almost done with one curtain, and I felt better about the next day, much better.

My day improved again markedly when I heard tires on the driveway and opened the door to see Santiago there with a bottle of white wine and some yellow tulips. He leaned over and kissed me gently before saying, "I really am sorry about earlier."

I smiled. "I know, and it's okay. It was an awkward moment for everyone, but I would love to hear, if you can tell me, about what Kyle said." I took the bottle of wine. "But first, we need to pour this and get those into some water."

Santiago smiled and went right to the cabinet where I kept my vases. He filled a blue-glass vase and, after cutting the stems, put the tulips inside and set the arrangement at the center of my table. It looked perfect, and I knew Sawyer would be excited to see "his plants" in the morning. He'd really taken to admiring flowers, and he loved to see them on the table.

Wine glasses in hand, we stepped out onto the porch into the soft chill of a spring night. I had put out our blankets, but neither of us needed them. Our sweatshirts, his with a simple brand logo in the upper corner and mine with a "I have two hobbies: buying cross-stitch supplies and actually cross-stitching," were enough warmth for the night, especially paired with the wine. It was a delicious Chardonnay.

He didn't even wait for me to ask. "Kyle is a suspect in his sister's murder."

I sighed. "He thought so. You think he killed her?"

"I have no idea, but it's common knowledge that she and he didn't get along, mostly because he held the same position about her identity as his parents did." He took a sip of his wine. "At least he once held that point of view."

"Yeah, he does seem to have changed, or at least he wants people to think he has." This was all so messy.

"Exactly. He told me he came to see you to offer to help with the memorial. Did you give him a job?" Santiago studied my face.

I shrugged. "I wasn't sure what the right thing to do was, so I did. He's going to help set up the shop with Mika. He said he and Trevor didn't get along, so I didn't think helping with the actual memorial was a good idea."

Santiago sat up. "I didn't know he and Trevor had clashed."

"Okay, let me see if I can fill you in." I told him about my conversation with Kyle and then the one I had with Ms. Nicholas. "A whole lot of secrets going around."

Santiago nodded and sat back. "I'll say. I knew Trevor

had a record, most of it from when he was a teenager, so nothing public, but I didn't know that Davenport had tried to have him arrested for kidnapping."

"That's odd, right? Were you not sheriff yet?"

"I wasn't sheriff, but I was a deputy at the time, I think. It is odd that I didn't know about it though, even if I came on after. That's a pretty big deal." He rubbed his chin. "Maybe they took it to a different jurisdiction?"

"Like the FBI. Isn't the FBI in charge of kidnapping cases?"

He chuckled. "The FBI does handle kidnapping cases if they cross state lines or if the victim is very young, but I was thinking more like they might have gone to Orange County."

I blushed. "Oh. Like they didn't think they'd get a fair hearing here."

"Maybe." He shrugged. "I'll look into it though. Thanks for the tip."

He put his hand, palm up, on the table between us, and I slid mine in. "Now, how are you doing?"

I looked out over the field in front of us and listened to the peepers sing for a minute. "Okay. A lot of people have been hurt here, most of all Celeste. But Trevor and maybe even her brother, too, since he absorbed what his parents said about his sister."

"Yeah," Santiago said as he rubbed his thumb over my knuckles. "We aren't going to fix all that, but we are doing what we can. You had the idea for a memorial."

"And you are going to find her killer." I picked up his hand and kissed it. "That will be our part."

"Exactly," he said.

We let the evening song surround us and talked of

simple things like the things I'd like to plant around the farmhouse and whether Sawyer could handle a miniature but fully functional excavator for his sandbox. It was a quiet moment, a much-needed quiet moment.

Chapter Seven

The next morning, Sawyer was up and at 'em with gusto.
Because he wanted to go out to his playground before we
left for his dad's house, he let me get him dressed and ate his
bacon and oatmeal without a fuss. Then, he was down and
climbing before I could even put on my sweater.

He was good and tuckered out for the ride. I handed
him a protein bar and his juice and reveled in his repeated
singing of "Twinkle, Twinkle Little Star" for the whole ride.
Each time he sang, "Diamond, diamond in the sky," I
smiled. He was such a delight.

But today, especially, I was glad he got to spend time with
his dad because it wasn't going to be an easy afternoon, even
without all the tension between the people who had known and
loved Celeste. Sawyer bounded from the car and headed for his
jungle gym at his dad's house as soon as I released him from his
seat. His dad and I talked a bit, and then I shouted an "I LOVE
YOU" and double-beeped as I headed out the driveway.

On the drive to town, I put on The Wailin' Jennys and

soaked in the harmonies and lyrics of these talented women. Something about great music always sorted something in my spirit. Today was no exception, and I needed all the sorting I could get.

When I parked in the small lot just up the street from Mika's shop, I saw Lucille's car and smiled. She had texted this morning to say she hoped she hadn't gone overboard with the food for the reception, and I couldn't wait to see what she had made.

I grabbed my garment bag with my simple black dress for the service from the back of the car and headed up the block. I was delighted to see, coming toward me, my friend Mary Johnson, and she had a huge bouquet of flowers in her hand. "It's so good to see you," I said as we both leaned forward and did that not-quite-hug thing that people do when their hands are full.

"Ms. Nicholas suggested you might use these flowers down here at the reception. Would that be alright?" she said.

"Yes, yes please." I opened the door for her, and as she stepped in past me, I asked, "You knew Celeste?"

"Sort of. I knew her the way we all know each other here. Enough to say hi." Mary set the flowers on the table. "Now, what else can I do?"

"I could use some help filling trays," I heard Lucille say from the back of the shop.

"There you go." I smiled. "I'll be back in a second. Just want to check in with Mika." My best friend was organizing her bins of yarn at the front of the shop, and since that was typically my Saturday job, I didn't want to leave her to it by herself. "Need some help?"

"Oh, thank you. Yes. I want the store to look perfect for

this afternoon." She hefted a huge box toward me. "Help me put out this new turquoise yarn?"

I took out a few skeins of the chenille and smiled. "This is gorgeous. I love the color."

"Me too, and I thought it would make the front of the store look bright but not garish for today." Mika began unloading one bin of muted gray, and I replaced those skeins with the turquoise. It looked lovely without, as Mika said, being too eye-catching.

We continued our way around the shop, refilling bins and adding "shelf enhancers." I was particularly fond of a pair of gargoyles I'd salvaged from a historic house that was undergoing a major renovation. The owners had let me take anything I wanted from the façade of the stone mansion, and I'd immediately grabbed these two hand-sized critters. They would make excellent bookends, and if they hadn't been prone to damage by toddler hands, I probably would have kept them for myself.

As we finished our last bins, Kyle Davenport came in and waved. I smiled and signaled for him to come over as I took a quick look at my watch. "Ooh, man, I need to get scooting. Let me introduce you to Kyle, and then I'll do a quick change in the back, if that's okay with you," I said.

Mika smiled and nodded. Then she turned to Kyle and put out her hand. "Kyle, glad you're here to help. Paisley here has to go do a Superman in the back room, but if you'll come with me, we can help get the rest of the food ready."

"Superman?" I heard Kyle say as they walked toward the tables, where Lucille's goodies were all set out.

When I came out, in tights but without the cape, Lucille smiled and said she'd walk over with me. "Looks like everything is under control here." We both waved at Kyle and

Mika as they arranged the cups and beverages one of Saul's crew had dropped off earlier along with a secret cooler of hard cider for us to drink later, when the crowd left.

As my stepmother and I headed the few blocks north to the historical society museum, I felt my nerves getting the better of me. I knew Trevor and Ms. Nicholas had put together a lovely service, and I was glad so many people were coming. But Celeste's parents would surely be there, and their presence alone would probably be disruptive. Add in the probable tension between Trevor and Kyle, and this could be a real powder keg of an afternoon.

"Has anyone told you what Celeste was like?" Lucille's question interrupted my thoughts, and I found myself grateful for the distraction.

I paused and thought through my conversations with her friends and family. "No, not much. I know she really liked to dance." I sighed. "I haven't really asked though. I was too caught up in how she died and the fact that there was so much controversy over her remains, I guess."

Lucille took my arm. "That makes total sense, and you had a lot to handle just getting the memorial started, much less managing all the personalities involved. I'm eager to hear what people say about her. Given that she was at a seventies-themed dance, I think it's safe to say that she, at least, knew how to have fun."

I laughed. "Indeed. Although dancing at the VFW hall isn't exactly the pinnacle of entertainment."

"It is here in Octonia," Lucille said with a laugh.

As we got close to the historical society building, I could see two patrol cars parked out front and Officer Winslow in her dress uniform on the front porch. She looked regal and official, not to mention intimidating. Somehow, though, I

83

didn't think anything was going to intimidate the Davenports.

We had about a half hour until the service began, and people were beginning to fill the folding chairs on the lawn. Trevor and Ms. Nicholas had decided, given the large response, that the building itself was too small, so they'd use the porch of the house as a sort of stage and allow people to sit outside.

Saul was busy unfolding more chairs around the side of the building and gave a two-fingered salute when he saw us. Lucille peeled off to go speak with him while I climbed the few steps to the porch to join Ms. Nicholas, who was testing the microphone. She gave me a quick hug and then whispered into my ear, away from the microphone. "Trevor isn't thrilled about Kyle coming, but he understands. You might want to speak to him, though, just to give him some modicum of peace about the situation if you can." She nodded toward the door of the house.

"Of course," I said, and heard my voice boom through the microphone. As I reddened to the color of a ripe strawberry, I stepped inside to look for Trevor.

I found him folding programs at the kitchen table near the back of the house. "Need some help?" I asked as I pulled out a chair.

He looked up, smiled, and nodded. "That would be great. I really didn't think this many people would come."

I sighed. "I was a little surprised, too, but a lot of people must have cared about Celeste." I picked up a pretty yellow program with Celeste's face printed in gray scale on the front and folded it in half.

"Some did, but a lot of these people are just here to be nosy." Trevor's mouth was a hard line. "They either want to see what the deal was with Celeste, or they're here to see what the Davenports will do."

I *tsk*ed. "Yeah, I think you're right. We're kind of disgusting, us humans."

Trevor smiled. "We kind of are. But still, I'm glad people are coming. I want people to know her."

As I folded, I thought about Lucille's question and started to ask him to tell me about Celeste. But then I remembered Kyle and decided I needed to tackle that conversation first. "Trevor, I know Ms. Nicholas told you Kyle Davenport is coming and that he's helping out with the reception. I wanted you to know that I did not intend to make any trouble—"

Trevor interrupted me. "I know, and I don't think there will be any. He posted a very nice comment on the event last night saying that he hoped people would respect Celeste and this memorial for her and that he would be there to honor his sister as she wanted to be honored." He took a deep breath. "It seems like he has really changed."

I smiled. "I hope so, but if he hasn't . . ." I didn't know what to say next.

"If he hasn't, then I won't be surprised, and we are prepared. A group of Celeste's friends will sit at the front, and we're all prepared to stand and form a sort of human wall if the Davenports get loud or try to move to the stage." Trevor's jaw was firm as he pressed a tight crease into the last program.

"The sheriff and Officer Winslow are here. Might it be best to let them handle things?" I felt nervous having people in the way of anyone whose hatred might make them interrupt a memorial service.

"Actually, the human wall was my idea," Santiago said from the doorway. "They've been used effectively for nonviolent protests for decades. A bunch of college kids formed one when the hate-mongers from Westboro Baptist came to protest their production of *The Laramie Project*, and it kept the protesters from getting to the actors and audience but also kept the actors and audience from reacting."

I nodded. I'd seen those walls of people wearing angel wings at events where people threatened violence against the LGBTQ+ community. "You think we're going to need that?" I asked.

"I hope not," the sheriff said as he casually slipped his arm around my shoulders, "but we trained this morning just in case."

I turned to look up into his face. "You did a training with Celeste's friends?"

Santiago nodded, and when I looked over at Trevor he was grinning.

"It was really great. Actually made us feel like we were honoring her by preparing to stand up for her, even if we don't have to do it," Trevor said as he stacked the programs and handed me a few dozen. "Will you help me distribute these?"

I choked back my tears. "Of course."

Trevor turned and headed out to the front lawn.

Before I followed him, I stretched to my tiptoes and kissed Santiago's cheek. "You look very nice today, and I'm very glad you're here." He, too, was in his dress uniform with a dark-brown jacket over a white shirt and brown tie. The look was discrete but sharp.

He squeezed me. "I'm glad you're here, too, and you look lovely."

I smiled and headed out to distribute programs to the few dozen people who had already arrived. It was going to be a large crowd indeed.

The next few minutes flew by as I passed out programs, greeted old friends, and tried to keep an eye out for the Davenports. At just a minute before one, I saw Kyle take a seat in the third row, and I smiled when Trevor went over and handed him a program. I didn't think they were ever going to be best friends, nor should Trevor be expected to even be more than generally kind to him, but it was nice to see an attempt at healing.

My flicker of good feeling faded quickly, though, when Mr. and Mrs. Davenport arrived. They came in a slick black town car and emerged from the back door like they were walking down a red carpet at some Hollywood premiere. I bit back a smile, though, as Mrs. Davenport's grand entrance was somewhat stymied when her stiletto heels stuck in the sod at the edge of the curb.

Saul came to her rescue and took her arm, an act to which she gave a patronizing nod. Her felicitousness quickly turned to ire, though, when Saul steered her away from the main seating area and led her to an empty row at the side of the building, near the back. At a loss for what to do but follow his wife and her new escort, Mr. Davenport trailed behind.

As Saul came to join me at our seats in the front of the building, I gave him a thumbs-up down by my knee. He squeezed my thumb as he sat down. I looked up at him and then over at Dad and Lucille on my other side. These people, my people, were good people. They were here because they believed in showing their appreciation for a young woman who had died too young, and they were here to support me.

I stared at the large photograph of Celeste that Trevor

had blown up and put beside the podium. It showed her with long blonde braids on either side of her beautiful face. She was laughing, and her chin was thrust up in the air. She looked joyful, and I wished so much that I had known her.

The service began with a young woman singing an a cappella version of "Morning Has Broken" that had me welling up before Trevor even got to the podium. But when Trevor began to speak about his friend, his vivacious, animal-loving, éclair-eating friend, I couldn't hold the tears back. It was clear he loved Celeste, and from the looks on most of the faces around me, many people shared his feelings or, at least, wished they had known her.

Another young woman spoke – Eva, I think her name was – and told a story about when Celeste had found a litter of kittens under the small house that sat just next to where we were now gathered. "The mother had been hit by a car, and Celeste didn't know if she could take the cats home because her mother was allergic. So, instead, she organized a round-the-clock feeding team who came every two hours to give the tiny kittens milk and to be sure they had warm hot-water bottles." Celeste had kept the kittens together until their eyes opened because she thought it was better to be surrounded by the ones you know in hard days. "Eventually, we raised enough money to get the kittens vaccines and have them spayed or neutered, and now, we all have these living reminders of Celeste sleeping on our couches."

Around the crowd, people stood up and held cats or cat carriers. It was a profoundly moving gesture, and I knew that I would tell Beauregard about it later. Even Beau would be touched by that story.

Just when I thought I would probably start sobbing audibly soon, a young woman stood and walked to the podium, where she recited "While Looking at Photo Albums," a poem by Kay Ulanday Barrett

> *I didn't get to –*
> *hold her hand as she died*
> *I said I tried*
> *just translates to*
> *I couldn't make it*
> *in time*
> *I tell myself*
> *ocean salt and tear salt*
> *are one and the same.*

I looked over at Mrs. Davenport, hoping I'd see tears, hoping I'd see sadness. But instead, all I saw was, well, nothing. She looked completely removed from the emotion of this moment. I decided to be gracious and think she had shut down because maybe she couldn't survive if she didn't.

The young woman sat down, and Ms. Nicholas stepped to the podium. Her remarks were brief but powerful. "When I learned of Celeste Davenport's death, I was saddened but determined. I had a mission as a historian to find out as much as I could about her death. That mission drove me, and I performed it well." She looked out at me and a small smile formed on her lips.

"But then, I learned that Trevor, the young man I call 'my boy,' was Celeste's dearest friend, that she trusted him so much that she asked him to act as her family in every sense, including legally." Mrs. Nicholas's eyes cut right toward where the Davenports were sitting, but she didn't turn her head. "Then, my determination turned to grief. I expect that is why many of you are here because your determination – to be Celeste's friend, to be her protector – has let go and become grief. I am glad you have come because grief shared is rich and powerful and full of story."

She held her hands out like she was giving a blessing, and perhaps she was. "May your grief be lifelong because deep love requires that. May your joy burst forth even so. May your stories heal us all."

With that, Celeste's friends stood, turned toward the crowd, and began to sing "Rise Up." Their voices were pitchy but strong, and I found myself pulled to my feet to try and sing along, even though I didn't know all the words to Andra Day's song. Soon, all of us were standing and singing, and it felt like Celeste could hear us, wherever she was now, and it felt like she was smiling.

As our last words echoed down the street, I felt that joy bursting forth, just like Ms. Nicholas said it might . . . and I was hopeful and happy.

Then, a shot pierced the silence, and when the second one came, we fell to the ground and screams drowned out the music.

––––––––––––––

Within minutes, Santiago and Officer Winslow had declared it safe, and those people who hadn't panicked and run began to get up and move around. Ms. Nicholas took the microphone again and said, "Please, everyone, join us for a quiet," – she looked meaningfully at Santiago, who nodded – "reception to honor Celeste at Stitch A Yarn."

Most people started to wander down the street, too shocked and emotionally overwhelmed to do anything else, I supposed. At least that's how I felt.

I made my way over to Santiago, with Dad and Lucille close behind. "Did you see who fired the shots?"

Santiago shook his head. "No, but they came from up on the hill." He gestured up to the abandoned plantation house behind us. "Winslow has gone up to investigate, but I suspect the shooter is long gone."

"Does she need help?" Saul asked as he joined us. "I mean, I'm not officially police, but I can look around."

"Actually," Santiago said, "I'd appreciate your presence there just to keep an eye out."

"I'll go with you," Dad said, and the two men walked casually up the hill, wise enough to move slowly and not make a scene.

Santiago took my hand and offered his arm to Lucille. "May I escort you two women?"

"A lovely offer, sir," Lucille said as she threaded her arm through his. "This way I can grill you. Who would have done that?"

"I have no idea. The likely suspects were all here." He shook his head.

"You mean the Davenports," I said.

He sighed. "Yes. But all three of them were in the crowd."

I looked around to see if I could find Kyle or his parents, but none of them were visible to me at the moment. "I saw them all there, too."

"Are we sure they were there the whole time, though?" Lucille asked. "I didn't really pay attention to them much, once we started singing."

Santiago sighed. "I had considered that, too. I didn't see them after everyone stood up, but I didn't see them leave either. I was at the edge of the crowd, though, so they could have slipped past me."

We had reached Mika's shop, and so I said, "Let me go see if Kyle is in here. I think I can ask him about the shots without making him nervous." I looked to Santiago. "Is that okay?"

"Yes, I'll be near the front door, though, okay? Have your phone in your hand just in case?"

I took out my phone and opened the screen to Santiago's contact page. I'd only need to push one button if I was in trouble. "Will do."

The crowd was thick as I came in, and I headed right for the food tables, thinking that Kyle would be helping Mika refill plates and hand out drinks. But neither of them was in sight. I did a quick spin around the store, but I couldn't find them.

I was just about to call Santiago in a panic to say that something had happened to Mika when she and Kyle emerged from the back room with their arms full of plates. I sighed and smiled before I walked over.

"Wild day, huh?" I said.

"Yeah, look at this crowd," Mika replied.

I frowned and looked at her. "Yeah, but this is only about half the people that came. You didn't hear the gunshots?"

Mika almost fumbled the plate of rugelach she was holding. "Gunshots? No! What gunshots?" She looked at me and then over to Kyle.

"Someone shot a gun at my sister's service?" Kyle asked.

I nodded and studied his face. "You were there."

He blinked and then said, "I left a little early to get over here and help."

Mika looked at me and then asked, "When did you leave?"

Kyle huffed and said, "I feel like I'm being interrogated, and I really don't think I need to answer that question." He turned away with his plate of snickerdoodles and stalked across the room.

I stared after him for a minute and then looked at Mika. "Well, that's not suspicious at all," I said.

Mika nodded. "He did get here several minutes before anyone else, so he must have left early."

"Early, yes, but all of us were prone or running for at least a couple of minutes after the shots were fired. He could have come from shooting toward the crowd straight here, and he still would have beat us all." I felt exhausted, and Kyle's defensiveness weighed heavy, especially since I'd trusted him.

"You okay here?" I asked Mika. When she nodded, I said, "I'll send Lucille over, but I need to find Santiago."

"I've got this. You go." She gave me a quick hug, and I scanned the room for the man in the bear-brown suit. He was near the front talking to a group of twenty-somethings, but when his phone rang, he raised it to his ear and found my face in the crowd.

"We need to talk," I said. "Back room?"

"On my way." I watched him long enough to see him say goodbye to the group around him and then turn to walk to the back.

I was just about to open the stockroom door when Kyle grabbed my arm, hard. "I need to talk to you," he said.

I turned to face him and said, "Kyle, I don't really have any desire to talk to you right now."

His face fell. "Okay. I just wanted to apologize. My therapist calls me 'hoity toity' when I get snippy and defensive like that. It's a bad habit." He sighed and said, "I'm sorry."

Just then, Santiago arrived at my shoulder and said, "Hi, Kyle." Then he looked at me. "Everything okay?"

"I think so," I said as I turned back to Kyle. "So do you want to tell us when you left the funeral?"

Santiago looked from me to Kyle.

"I left when they started singing 'Rise Up.' I was already crying, and I knew if listened to that song I'd break down." He took a shuddering breath. "I couldn't let my parents see that. They don't do well with weakness."

My heart broke for this young man, even if I was still miffed at him. "I see what you mean about a bad habit. It must be hard to always have everything under control."

Kyle's eyes filled with tears. "It really is." He cleared his throat and said, "But I didn't hear any gunshots. I practically ran here so that I could distract myself."

Santiago nodded. "Okay, well, thanks for explaining. You understand, though—"

"I will gladly take a gunpowder residue test, if you want?" Kyle said.

The sheriff cracked up laughing. "Well, I left my CSI: kit back at the station, but I will be asking people about when you left and if they saw you anywhere else. Okay?" He was still smiling.

Kyle's face softened. "Okay. I did pass a lot of people." He paused and looked over Santiago's shoulder. "Actually, she saw me running, asked if I was okay." He pointed to a woman standing near the door.

I smiled. "Ah, that's my friend Mary. We may be able to clear this up right now."

"Stay in the building, though. I'll let you know when you are free to go," Santiago said.

"I'm not going anywhere. The least I can do for Celeste is serve her cookies." He turned back toward the storeroom with his almost-empty plate.

"Mind if I tag along?" I said to Santiago.

"Never," he said as he slipped my hand into the crook of his arm.

"Never?" I said with a sly grin.

"Okay, almost never. I expect I can't have you along on interrogations." He winked.

Mary greeted us warmly and said she was sorry to have missed the service. "Funerals are hard for me." Mary had lost her teenage son a few years earlier, and just the idea of being at a funeral if Sawyer had died left me breathless. I could completely understand how she didn't want to attend this one.

"Understood. Just glad you're here now," I said. "Lucille baked."

Mary laughed. "I can see that. Those no-bake cookies look amazing, and I'm on my way to get one . . . or three."

"Mind if I ask you a question first?" Santiago said.

"Not at all, but the way you said that makes me think this isn't a request for my pork chop recipe?" She smiled, but her eyes looked sharp.

"Well, I definitely want that, too," he said, "but today, I'm wondering if you can tell me if you passed anyone just as Celeste's memorial was ending."

Mary looked up at the ceiling for a minute and then said, "I did, actually. Thought it was odd that someone was running in a tie, but to each his own."

"Do you see that man in this room?" Santiago asked.

"Now, I feel like I'm on one of those courtroom dramas," Mary quipped before looking around.

"Yep, he's the young man by the table with Mika. Handsome fellow." She studied Kyle for a minute. "He looks familiar, now that I see him at a slower speed." She smiled again.

"That's Kyle Davenport," I said. "Celeste's brother."

Mary nodded. "That's right. I recognize him from their family portrait that hangs at the senior center. They donated the money for the building."

I sighed. "Of course they did. Does that portrait, by chance, have just Kyle, or Kyle and Celeste too?"

Mary's face hardened. "It's actually of the four of them, but when the children were younger." She swallowed hard. "Oddly, though, the portrait was just commissioned and donated two years ago."

I growled. "So they painted a portrait of their missing child as that child was when they approved of her?"

Mary nodded. "I tried to get them to update the portrait, use more recent photos, but they kept saying they wanted to show their family members in their 'real form.'"

I swallowed back the mouthful of bile that rose in my throat and then had to grasp Santiago's arm tightly as I saw the Davenports stroll into Mika's shop like the king and queen of the room.

My eyes met Kyle's across the shop floor, and he looked terrified, and apparently for good reason because his mother stepped forward and said, "Thank you all for gathering to honor our child. We are here to tell you about him, the real him."

Chapter Eight

Fortunately, Mika was quick on her feet because before Mrs. Davenport could say another word, Mika charged forward, took both of the Davenports by the arm, and spun them back toward the door.

"You are not welcome here," Mika said. I stepped up next to her and felt Santiago just behind me.

"We were invited by Ms. Nicholas at the memorial service," Mrs. Davenport said in a silky, smooth voice that dripped with patronizing ick as she and her husband turned back to face the room.

"Well, I am uninviting you," Mika said. "You need to leave."

"I'm afraid we can't do that. This is a public event, and we are part of the public," Mr. Davenport said in a booming voice that carried across the room, the room that was now eerily silent.

"Actually, yes I can. I can refuse service to anyone I choose. You may remember when that bigoted bakery owner won his Supreme Court case to say he wouldn't make a wedding cake for a gay couple. That same cake means I can kick transphobic monsters out of my store. Now, leave!" Mika stomped her foot for impact, and the Davenports actually flinched.

Santiago stepped forward. "You heard the woman. Please leave before I have to escort you off the property."

The Davenports scowled at each of us in turn. Then, Mrs. Davenport caught sight of her son and said, "Come, Kyle. We are not welcome here."

I glanced at Mika, who nodded, and said, "Actually, Kyle is quite welcome. He is honoring his sister."

Mika smiled and pointed toward the door. "Please go," she said.

The Davenports looked, for the first time, actually flustered, but they turned, in unison, with a flourish and went out the door to their waiting car. Clearly, they had only wanted to make a scene and leave, and they had succeeded. But instead of causing an uproar, they brought out solidarity. As soon as their car pulled away, the entire room erupted in a cheer.

I felt exuberant, too, but the memory of those two gunshots was still pretty front-of-mind for me. So I spent most of the rest of the afternoon refilling plates of cookies and making sure the soda and punch didn't run out. I just wasn't up for small talk. By the time the last of the guests left around four, I was exhausted and my feet ached. I was not used to wearing any sort of heel, and my toes were reminding me of that.

I plopped into a wingback chair in the cozy corner and sighed as Mika and then Lucille dropped next to me. We'd just finished cleaning up, and the men were, true to gender stereotype, taking out the trash. I really wanted to hear what, if anything, Dad and Saul had found up on the hill behind the society house, but first, I wanted a cider.

Mika had set the cooler between us, and we each opened a can and sat back. "I'm glad Trevor and Ms. Nicholas made it down for a bit," Mika said after taking a long draw out of her can.

"Me, too, but I'm also glad they got waylaid until after the Davenports' nonsense. Trevor doesn't need to be subjected to any more of that," I said.

"Agreed," Lucille said as she lifted her can. "To Trevor."

"To Trevor," Mika and I toasted.

"And to Kyle," I said more quietly. "It can't have been easy for him to see his parents behave that way, and on today of all days."

Mika sighed. "I expect he's used to it, which is sad on an entirely different level."

Kyle had stayed around to clean up, but once we got the few cookies that were left packed into containers for Santiago to take back to the station, he headed out after saying thank-you many times for letting him participate. He hadn't said where he was going, but I really hoped it was somewhere with friends.

Santiago, Dad, and Saul came back in the back door and joined us for cider and a few surprise beers that Saul had slipped into the cooler.

"Robard was very pleased with the service," Saul said. "He thought Celeste was honored well."

"He was there?" I asked. "I didn't see him."

Saul nodded. "He was there, sent me a text to say he was glad to see me there, too. But he didn't want to show his face. Apparently, he and Mr. Davenport have had a few run-ins over the years."

"Is there anyone the Davenports haven't put off in Octonia?" I asked.

Santiago tilted his head, smiled, and said a simple "no."

All of us chuckled at that before the mood grew darker again. I kind of just wanted to sit and relax with my friends and family, but I knew I wouldn't rest until I heard if Dad and Saul had found anything.

Dad must have had the same feeling because he pulled a small baggie out of his pocket. "Found these up the hill, Sheriff. Sorry I didn't have anything more official to put them in." He handed the bag over to Santiago.

"Shotgun shells. That explains the big booms," Santiago said.

"And why no one got hit with any bullets," Saul added. "The shot didn't go that far."

Santiago nodded. "Yeah. Didn't happen to see any shot up there, did you?"

I leaned forward as I remembered my dad teaching me to shoot a shotgun when I was fourteen. He'd wanted me to understand how the gun worked, to see how far projectiles would fly. Even then, I hated guns, even though I got a strange thrill from firing something so powerful. The lesson stuck, though, and I was able to understand the conversation now for it. "You're thinking they used buckshot?"

Dad nodded. "It would make sense. It's the thing most people around here would have on hand. But the thing is, we didn't find any shot pellets where we should have. Not embedded in trees or on the ground either."

"You think the shells were at the shooting location?" Santiago asked.

Saul nodded and said, "Looked like it. The grass was mashed down, but it looked like they shot directly toward the back of the Bel Grove house."

"But that façade is brick," I said. "The pellets could have ricocheted back on them."

"Not if they didn't have any shot in the shells," Saul said and looked at Santiago.

"They were firing blanks," Santiago said. "Just to scare us."

Dad and Saul both nodded. "That's what we think. The part we can't figure out," Dad said, "is why."

"Terrorism," Mika said. "They just wanted to scare people."

"Yeah, that's true," Santiago said. "But why at this event? What purpose did that serve?"

"Isn't it enough reason for a psychopath to want to instill fear?" I asked and winced at the hyperbole of my own words. "Sorry. Long day. But I mean, couldn't the fear be reason enough?"

Santiago shrugged, "Maybe. But most of the time, actions like this are about distraction. So what might someone have wanted to distract us from? That's the question I think we all need to consider."

I dropped back in my seat. "I feel like I'm considering a lot these days. Can I consider tomorrow instead?"

Santiago smiled and stood before walking over to help me to my feet. "Yes, definitely. What do you say we have a barbecue instead? My place?"

"Are you grilling?" Dad asked as he and Lucille stood. "Because I'll need to supervise if you are. There's a certain knack to grilling burgers, you know?" Dad winked.

"Who said anything about burgers? I have steaks for us all. Who's in?" Santiago smiled as every hand went up.

He gave out the address and then took my hand. "You're riding with me," he ordered playfully.

"Absolutely. But first, I need to put myself back into my

comfy clothes. Give me five?" I said as I moved toward the back room.

He smiled and sat back down.

When I came out, Saul had already left to go get more beer, and Dad and Lucille were helping Mika close up the store. I shrugged on my paisley flannel shirt over my T-shirt. "Ready," I said. "Also, I like baked potatoes with my steak." I took Santiago's hand.

"Of course, and fresh asparagus," he said. "That's the only way to do it." He kissed my cheek, and we all headed out.

I had never been to Santiago's house before, and I was eager to see it. He'd mentioned me coming over before, but with Sawyer, it was usually simply easier for him to come to our house. Now, though, I stood in his yard and smiled. The house was a simple brick ranch, but around it was the most luscious landscape I'd ever seen. Even Dad was speechless.

Large, mulched beds housed rhododendrons under just-blooming maple trees, and the sunny faces of daffodils shone everywhere. In the raised beds in front of the house, not-yet-blooming tulips sat next to purple and white Lenten roses. When we walked around back, Santiago's deck was edged in pots full of herbs, and a large garden of freshly tilled earth sat partially planted. Tiny white tags were labeled *lettuce*, *spinach*, and *peas*.

I found myself wondering if Santiago would mind plying his landscape and gardening skills at the farmhouse this year, and maybe for years to come. But I pushed such silliness out of my mind and followed him up onto the deck. He lit one of those tall propane heaters that restaurants use on their patios and then asked Dad and Saul to help him get the food ready inside. Dad and Saul exchanged a look, and I heard Dad mumble something about women's work as he went inside. But Santiago just winked as he handed me a glass of white wine. "You three rest," he said.

I smiled and said, "If it's okay with you, I'll take a walk around the yard."

"Make yourself at home," he said before he closed the French doors behind him. I was eager to see the inside of his house and hoped it was as lovely as the outside, but for now, I'd relish the time with my two favorite women and explore the yard.

At the edge of the woods at the back of the lot, a small bank of snowdrops was dancing in the evening breeze. As I walked further along, I could see the green tips of daylilies emerging and the stiff spikes of irises, too. His yard was going to be a spark of floral color all spring, and I so hoped I'd get to see it.

"He has a very green thumb," Lucille said, and I nodded. I liked a man who enjoyed yard work. I liked that man a lot.

"I can separate some of those daylilies and irises for you in the fall, if you want," Santiago called from where he was sitting on the deck.

I smiled, both at the offer of flowers for the farmhouse and because he thought we'd be doing things like that in the fall. "I'd love that," I shouted.

Mika took my other arm and said, "He's a good one, Pais." She looked me in the eye and nodded.

I felt myself welling up a little because it had been a while since I'd had a "good one," but I thought she was right. Still, I wasn't in a hurry to move things faster than they were going. It was nice to just let things evolve, to not feel like I had to control the situation. We would get where we were going in our own time.

Lucille, Mika, and I made our way back up to the deck and joined the men. "Potatoes will be a while," Santiago said, "so we can all relax for a bit."

A long, soft silence settled over us as we sipped our drinks. I enjoyed the contrast between the warmth of the heater and the crispness of the evening spring air. It was like a bonfire without all the physical labor.

After a while, Mika said, "It seems like people thought Celeste's service was lovely. Well, until the shooting, that is."

Dad nodded. "It was a nice service. I was glad a lot of people came out for it."

"Me, too," I said. "But I do wish Mr. and Mrs. Davenport had stayed away."

Saul looked at me. "Do you? I was actually glad they came. They got to see people appreciate their daughter for who she was, not who they wanted her to be. That might have been good for them."

Lucille sighed. "I had the same thought until they showed up at Mika's shop trying to 'manage the message.'" Between her air quotes and the edge to her voice, my stepmother made her feelings about their outburst very clear.

Mika rubbed her hands together and scooted a little further under the heater. "I really wish they hadn't done that. It would have been far better for them to come in, mingle, and if they felt it necessary, spread their nonsense quietly."

"That's not the Davenport way, though," Dad said. "They are loud and brash. It's just how they get things done." My dad had a way of being honest that was both kind and sort of stunning.

"It is," Saul agreed. "Still, I'm always hopeful people can be better. Do better."

This time the silence wasn't as easy, but it was still nice to be with my people on a beautiful night. I missed Sawyer, always did when he was away, but I also appreciated this time with just adults.

"Any progress on the investigation, Sheriff?" Saul asked.

Santiago took a long pull from his beer bottle and shook his head. "Not much, I'm afraid. I can't say a lot, but the suspects we had don't look good for it. Honestly, the cause of death isn't clear, and aside from the very obvious possibility of fear and hatred, we don't have a clear motive."

Lucille asked, "So you don't think she was killed because she was trans?"

"I don't know," Santiago said with a shrug. "That might have been the reason, but it could have been anything else, too."

"But she was placed so carefully there in the warehouse. Doesn't that give you something to go on?" Mika asked.

"It does. It's likely the killer knew her and felt some remorse for their actions or wanted her to be at peace." He sighed. "This is the strangest case I've ever worked. Usually, it's pretty straightforward, but this one . . ."

I looked out over Santiago's beautiful yard and thought about the warehouse, about the objects we'd seen there, and about the way someone had taken care to not only hide Celeste's body but also to be sure it was protected from animals and the elements. "The warehouse has to matter, doesn't it? I mean, that was a place Celeste loved. The person who put her there had to know that, right?"

Santiago nodded slowly. "Yes. I think so. But that could be anyone who knew her, really, especially since the warehouse has been empty for so long. It wouldn't have taken a lot of planning to get her body there, even with the work required to move all those bags of soil."

I nodded. "I'm sure you've thought of this, but the person who put her there had to have known the building, too, right? Otherwise, they wouldn't have been aware of the elevator shaft in the basement. It's not really that obvious back in the corner where it sits."

"True," Saul added. "I only saw it because I wanted to be sure to check every part of the building before we started to take it down. It's not good to have surprises at a demolition site."

"Right, and honestly, not something I had considered from quite that angle." Santiago massaged his neck. "I'll look into that a bit more. Thanks."

He stood. "You up for helping me set the table?" he asked me. "It's getting a bit too chilly to eat out here, I think."

"Sure," I said as I took the hand he offered and let him pull me to standing. "Plus, I get to see inside your house." I winked.

"This is not one of your salvage jobs, Paisley Sutton," Dad said with a smile. "No snooping."

Santiago draped his arm around my shoulders and whispered in my ear so only I could hear. "You can snoop all you want, Woman."

I blushed and stepped inside a small space with a dining table next to a peninsula off the galley kitchen. But what it lacked in size it made up for in charm. All the mid-century characteristics that some people loved had been stripped away, and instead, the house looked like a charming Craftsman bungalow with lots of simple wood trim and earth tones in the fabric and the wall colors. "Santiago, your house is beautiful," I whispered.

He smiled. "I've done a lot of work to make it to my taste. I like where I live to feel comfortable, not sterile."

"It really is so cozy," I said as I walked past the rustic farm table into a living room with a low-slung couch and two armchairs arranged so people could chat or watch TV on the small screen over the fireplace. The bay window behind the sofa had been trimmed out in straight-cut boards, and it was filled to overflowing with house plants. "And you really like plants," I said with a smile.

"I really do. I don't have any pets because my job is so unpredictable, but I like caring for things. Plants give me that chance." He stood behind me in the small doorway to the other side of the kitchen. "Why don't you do some *snooping* while I prep the steaks?"

I grinned. "You really don't mind?"

"Not a bit. Make yourself at home," he said again.

I decided I would do just that and turned left to go down the hallway there. A small bathroom was decorated with photographs of tree trunks and wildflowers, and the bedroom across the hall had been converted into a tidy office with a small secretary's desk and a built-in bookcase.

Further down, I stepped into what must have been a guest bedroom. The comforter was a simple dark green, and mismatched but coordinated lamps stood on rustic tables on either side of the headboard. At the foot of the bed, a window looked out on the backyard, and in one corner, an antique Martha Washington sewing cabinet held a copy of Thoreau's *Walden* and a set of towels. He was ready for guests, and I liked that.

But it was the room across the hall that I was really eager to see. When I stepped in, I took a deep breath and let Santiago's scent of sandalwood and aftershave waft over me as I looked at his queen-sized bed with a simple off-white duvet and two pillows covered in blue-plaid flannel. An antique-looking dresser stood to one side, but I resisted my snooping tendencies and didn't open the drawers to look at the joints so I could date the piece . . . or peek at what he kept there. Beyond the dresser, there was a small en suite bathroom.

I made my way to the other side of the bed, where a lamp and a stack of books sat. All of them were about birds or gardening, and for a brief second, I imagined myself lying in bed next to him while he told me about what he was going to plant next.

Quickly, though, I shook off that image and made my way to the kitchen. "It really is lovely, Santiago. Simple, and so very comfortable."

"Thank you," he said as he turned from the sink and dried his hands on the towel. "I'm really glad you like it." He leaned forward and kissed me softly.

I sighed and sank into him for just a minute before pulling away to say, "Now, where do I find plates?"

He smiled and pointed to a cabinet. I took out six stoneware plates and opened drawers until I found the silverware. Santiago grabbed six mason jar glasses and paper napkins. Soon, the table was set, and we went back out to the deck.

Santiago, under Dad and Saul's careful supervision, grilled the steaks and asparagus to perfection, and we enjoyed a wonderful dinner while we talked about our favorite TV shows and whether or not the new shopping center in town was a good idea. Most of us were of the opinion that we'd love a few more amenities, especially if the businesses were locally owned, but that we hoped no chains came in.

It was a perfectly lovely evening, and while I was a bit

sad when it ended, I was also happy to know we'd do it again soon. Santiago drove me home, and we enjoyed a lingering kiss on my porch before I went inside, fed Beauregard, and dropped into a deep sleep almost immediately.

I woke in the night, though, after a dream about tripping into a large elevator shaft and falling into a flower bed. As I sat up to shake the dream away, I felt a pull of worry. Robard Greene knew that warehouse inside and out, and I didn't like to think what that meant.

Chapter Nine

The next morning, after a few more hours of fitful sleep, I pulled myself out of bed and got ready for church. Anxiety tingled under my skin, and I needed the company of friends and good music more than ever.

I'd been attending Bethel Church for a few months now, and although I was one of a handful of white people who went there, the people of Bethel had made me feel completely at home. That morning when I arrived, Sister Harriet hugged me and asked after Sawyer, and Mr. Lexington handed me a loaf of his infamous zucchini bread. "Used the last of my frozen stash for this batch," he said with a wink.

I made my way to *my* seat next to Mary and squeezed her hand as I sat down. I'd come early, as was my habit, because I just liked to be in the sanctuary to hear the bustle and conversation of everyone coming in. It felt like being part of a large family that was simply going about their business.

"Long day yesterday," Mary said as she turned toward me in the pew.

"So long, but it ended well." I told her about going to Santiago's house and how lovely it was.

Mary smiled. "Somehow, I didn't expect our sheriff to be such a homemaker."

"Me neither. I mean I thought he'd have a tidy, sturdy house, but that was a real surprise." It was calming to just be here, talking about Santiago, with a friend.

We sat and listened to the organist do his exuberant warm-ups for a bit, and then Mary said, "That was a wild hour after the service, huh?"

I sighed. "It was. Between the shooting and the Davenports, it felt a bit like we were living in a TV drama."

She chuckled. "There's always drama in Octonia. But the Davenports do bring it to new heights." Mary stared up at the cross behind the pulpit for a minute. "I always thought she'd mellow out a bit."

"Who, Mrs. Davenport? You know her?"

"Well, as much as you know anyone you went to school with." She smiled. "I wouldn't say we were friends, but yeah, we knew each other."

I thought about it, and it made sense. Octonia only had one high school, and so all of us went to school with everyone our age. "She was, um, intense in high school too?" I was trying to be kind since we were in church, but *intense* wasn't exactly my first choice of words to describe Mrs. Davenport.

"Oh yes. Not just captain of our cheerleading squad but also drum major for the marching band." Mary chuckled. "It was kind of fun to watch her run around like a chicken with her head cut off at halftime, I will admit."

"That seems ambitious," I said remembering my own

frenzy to do all the things in order to get into a good college. I had loved the running between meetings and practices, but now just the thought of all that *going* made me tired.

"She was ambitious. Still is." Mary glanced over at me. "You know she's running for Octonia Board of Supervisors this fall, right?"

I turned and stared. "No, I didn't know that." I thought about it for a minute. "Makes sense, though. She seems like she'd like a life in politics, even small-town ones."

Mary nodded. "She has a plan to bring in high-speed internet and city water."

"I'm all for internet, but city water? For what? The twenty houses in town?" It made no sense to have a central water system for our town because, aside from the few shops on Main Street, the town of Octonia really only had a couple of dozen homes. All of them had wells, as did the businesses.

"Well, her house is one of those twenty, right?" Mary said with a raised eyebrow.

I shrugged. "Sure, but then she'd have to pay for water. If she already has a well, she's not paying anything now. Why do that?"

Mary tilted her head and looked at me like I was being dumb, and then it hit me. "She wants to expand the town, put in developments," I whispered.

"Exactly. A friend at VDOT told me that she's already applied for road changes at three plots of land around town. All property she owns." Mary made a popping sound with her mouth. "She stands to make a lot of money."

The events of the past few days started to fall into a pattern like dominos. Mrs. Davenport didn't want Celeste's death to hurt her chances of winning that seat on the board, and she knew that if it looked like she supported her trans daughter, the bigots here in Octonia – of which there were sadly many – wouldn't vote for her. And then she wouldn't be able to push through her development plans. "What a despicable woman, to use her daughter's death that way."

Mary sighed. "Well, she always has been driven."

Fortunately, the organist started up full-force with his rendition of "I'll Fly Away," and I was swept up in the music sufficiently enough to quell the churning of anger in my chest. I would think about Mrs. Davenport and her ugliness later.

The pastor gave a rousing sermon about love, about how important it is to remember that we are beloved just as we are. I thought of Celeste, of the way she had embraced who she was made to be, and then I thought of myself, of how I was finally coming to understand that no matter how well or how poorly I acted, God still loved me. And when the choir started to sing "Just As I Am," I sang with conviction and hope.

After the service, I spent a lovely afternoon with Mary and some other church friends, and they taught me to play bridge. I knew I was going to forget the rules as soon as I left the house, but for those couple of hours, I took to the game like a fish to water and dominated. Around four, when Mary sent me home with a second slice of lemon meringue pie, I was feeling good and confident.

Beauregard was less than pleased that I had not been on hand to tend to his many needs for a few hours, so I appeased him by putting his blanket in the dryer for a few minutes and then stretching it out beside me on the couch while I ate my pie for dinner. When I got out my sewing and settled in to watch *Blown Away* and stitch, he curled against me and purred. A purr was a rare gift from this guy, so I did my best to not need to get up.

Sawyer came home about six and was all words and energy, so he flew around the yard for a while with me trailing and listening. Then, it was time for some steam train videos, a bit of hide-and-seek, and a quick collapse into bed for my little guy.

Once he was settled, I picked back up my sewing room kit and started to stitch a thimble as my thoughts floated back to Mrs. Davenport's scheme. I found myself saddened and disappointed by her plans, but more, I was enraged that she would use her daughter's death and memorial service to forward her own agenda. She was deplorable.

Before I let my anger take over and make me lose perspective, I knew I needed to let Santiago know. It was early evening, and so I thought Beau might tolerate it if Santiago came over later. I texted him, told him I had some info to share, and wondered if we might get together tonight.

See you at nine? he replied almost immediately.

Perfect. Bring Kahlua. Tonight I needed a White Russian, my favorite mixed drink. It would make for a sweet end to a lovely day but a hard weekend. Besides if I was going to keep my anger at Mrs. Davenport in check, I needed something to take the edge off, and the apple juice in the refrigerator was not going to cut it.

Prompt as always, Santiago knocked quietly at nine and said, "Come around front. I have a small surprise." He turned to walk back off the side porch before looking over his shoulder and saying, "Bring the milk and tumblers."

I smiled and picked up my tray that was already prepared

with our supplies. When I came around the side of the house, I saw a small fire in a corner of the yard. It was ringed with stones that I thought had probably come from the pile that had once been the old kitchen chimney. A while back, I had mentioned to Santiago that I wanted a firepit, and now, he had made a makeshift one – we'd need to dig a hole for a real one before we could do anything sizeable – but this was perfect for tonight.

"You've been here a while," I said as I slid the tray onto the little table he'd brought down from the porch with our chairs.

"I thought we could both use a little extra light tonight," he said as he chucked another log from the small pile beside him onto the flames. "You can hear Sawyer from here okay?"

I looked back to where I'd left the inside door open and knew that my son would make himself heard. "I can. Thanks."

He picked up a bottle of Kahlua from beside his chair and mixed our drinks before handing me mine and saying, "Here's to a quiet day." Then he leaned over and looked closely at my face. "It was quiet, right?"

I smiled. "It was." I told him about church and playing bridge, but then I let the silence descend. "I did hear something at church, though. Something you need to know, if you don't already."

He sighed. "Okay, just give me one second." He took a long sip of his drink and then said, "Hit me."

"Did you know Mrs. Davenport—" I interrupted myself. "What is her first name anyway? I feel like I'm giving her too much respect by calling her 'Mrs. Davenport' all the time."

"Creedence."

I spit my drink to the fire. "Excuse me? Did you say *Creedence*? As in *Clearwater Revival*?"

"I did. That is her first name." Santiago smiled over his tumbler.

"Alright then, did you know Creedence is running for the board of supervisors this fall?"

"I did. She has made a few attempts at winning my support these past few weeks, although I think our inter-change when I notified them that we had discovered Celeste's body might have stopped that hopeless endeavor."

"Well, good. Okay, then did you know she already has plans submitted to VDOT for new intersections at housing developments she wants to build around town?" I was really hoping this wasn't news because I did not want to burden him with anything else.

The way his glass hung suspended near his chin told me that I'd caught him off-guard, though, and I sighed. "You didn't know."

He shook his head. "I didn't know. But now that you say that, it doesn't surprise me. How did you hear about this?"

I told him what Mary had heard and about the locations she mentioned, three large plots of farmland on three different sides of Octonia proper. "She said the plans submitted for traffic and roadway considerations would allow for five hundred or more houses right near town."

"That would bring more than ten times more people to town. We don't even have a stoplight. What is she thinking?"

I rubbed my fingers together in the universal symbol for *cash*, and Santiago hurled another log into the fire.

"I suppose that's it. Ugh." He slid down in his chair and drained his drink. "So now, she's even more of a suspect."

I looked over at him. "She is. You see these situations as related?"

"Maybe." He stared into the fire for a few moments before continuing. "Go with me on this, okay?"

I nodded. "Sure."

"A woman with political ambitions discovers her child is trans. Because this woman lives in a culturally conservative area, she realizes her child's identity might be a major road-block to her goals."

I groaned. "So she could have killed Celeste to remove the hindrance some people might see a trans child to be." I wanted to cry again. "But wouldn't it have simply been possible for her to do what she's doing now and deny who Celeste really was? She could have effectively divorced her child and accomplished the same thing, right?"

Santiago stared at the fire for a few seconds. "Probably, but there are those who toss around words like 'abomina-tion' with abandon."

I shuddered. "I can't imagine how a mother could kill her own child." I said the words, and I meant them, even as I realized that mothers killed their children all the time. It wasn't a rare occurrence, but when I pictured that little boy upstairs asleep, I could not conceive of anything he could do or be in this world that would make me even able to entertain the idea of ending his life.

Santiago rubbed his neck. "But of course, if this is the motive, it leaves us with two more suspects who also shared that motivation."

"Kyle and Mr. Davenport."

"Stephen," Santiago said before I could ask.

"So it could be Creedence, Stephen, or Kyle Daven-port," I said and groaned. "This gets more and more sad."

He nodded. "I don't think it's Kyle, of course, but I've learned I can be wrong. I just hope I'm not this time."

The White Russian had stopped easing my discomfort, and I set the watered-down third of the drink on the table. "I did think of something last night, but I hope I'm just worrying things to nonsense," I said quietly.

Santiago reached over and took my hand. "So far, I've seen no nonsense from you at all."

I chuckled. "Oh, I'm full of nonsense, for sure, but I try not to manufacture it – social media and reality TV do enough of that." I felt the weight of my suspicion as I spoke. "Have you considered Robard Greene?"

Santiago stood up, moved the table between us, and set his chair next to mine before pulling my hand into his lap and rubbing the fingers of his right hand over my knuckles as my hand rested in his left one. "Again, I hope I'm right and that it's not him. But yes. What made you think of him?"

I told him about how it had occurred to me that the person who hid Celeste's body must have known the building well. "It seems like he must know the building better than anyone."

"Except maybe Celeste herself," he added as he cupped my hand in both of his. "Is it terrible for me to say that if someone had to murder that poor woman, I hope I find it was Creedence or Stephen Davenport?"

"I totally understand, but I'd keep that one between you and me," I said as I leaned over to kiss his cheek. I let the silence sit around us for a bit before I said, "So what do you do now? I know you can't tell me specifics, but I'm just asking as more of . . ." I held up our clasped hands in lieu of the word *girlfriend*, which seemed so eleventh grade.

He smiled. "Too old fashioned to say 'my intended,' I suppose."

I felt heat rush to my face, and I wanted to have a pithy response about all that being dependent on what exactly he intended. Instead, I just smiled.

"I follow the leads. I haven't yet talked to the folks who put on the VFW dances, but since it seems likely that she died after one of them, I need to talk to the men there." He stared into the fire a moment before he said, "Saul is a vet, right?"

I nodded. "Vietnam. You thinking of taking him along to the VFW?"

"I am. These guys know me, but it's always better if one of their own vouches for me. Think he'd go?"

I laughed. "Are you serious? Saul likes to pretend he's all nonchalant and distant, but he's as nosy as the rest of us."

"Cool. After that, I want to sit down with Ms. Nicholas and Trevor to get their thoughts based on what they found in their research."

"And what Trevor knew of Celeste, I expect?"

"Exactly." He let go of my hand to throw the last piece of wood into the flames. "Then, if I don't find a more firm direction, I bring people in for formal questioning."

I sighed. "That doesn't sound like fun."

"It's not, and despite what they show on television, it's the hardest row to hoe, especially this long after the fact. People have had years to firm up their stories, and by now, they probably even believe those stories." He stood up and stretched.

"Whew. That does sound hard. Well, I'm going to hope the old-timers at the VFW can help, for what it's worth." I smiled and stood.

"It's worth a lot," he said as he pulled me closed and kissed me breathless.

The next morning, Saul called bright and early to let me know that he was headed to the VFW hall for bingo with Santiago but that we were cleared to go into the warehouse. "I can't have a crew there until the afternoon, but if you and your young sidekick want to go tag things to haul over to your space at the yard, you can do that this morning. I can have a truck and a loading crew over there by one."

I smiled as I said that sounded like a great plan. When I told Sawyer we were going on an adventure, he said, "For pizza?" and I had to laugh.

Fortunately, he was quite willing to explore a building, so we were loaded up with a grumpy Maine Coon in a half hour. The building looked just the same as the last few times I'd seen it, but now it felt different. The fact that Celeste had lain there for more than five years made it more a graveyard than anything else to me.

A small patch of daffodils had naturalized in the area near the front door, and Sawyer and I picked a handful each. Then, we went around the back of the building, opened the combination box which held the key, using the code Saul had given me, and let ourselves in. I led Sawyer in the direction of the elevator shaft so that we could leave our flowers at Celeste's resting place. But as we approached, I stopped short.

The entire place was filled with lit candles and flowers, and in the center, the photo of Celeste from the memorial sat, her face still alit with joy, and I found my heart racing with fear.

Chapter Ten

It was appallingly difficult to pull Sawyer away from all that flame, and I had to physically remove his screaming body while also dialing Santiago. Fortunately, as the call connected, Sawyer got distracted by the large pile of sand behind the building and started climbing while I filled Santiago in.

In minutes, he and Officer Winslow were back on the scene, and Dad was on his way to get Sawyer because I knew – for the sake of my statement but also my spirit – that I needed to stay there. While we waited for the police to examine the scene, Sawyer and I walked down the hill and looked at the trillium peeking out of the leaf fall. He found a superb stick and whacked some trees, and when I heard tires on the gravel above, we hiked back up so he could show his Boppy the mushroom he found. "Don't eat this, Boppy," he said with a wag of his finger. "It'll make your tummy hurt."

Dad smiled and admired the mushroom before he coaxed my son into the car with the promise of a picnic and a playground. Dad gave me a quick hug, and I kissed Sawyer on his pillow-soft cheek before watching them pull away.

Then, I let myself collapse against my car and cry for just a minute. The shrine was so beautiful . . . and absolutely terrifying.

After a moment, I pulled myself together and went back around the warehouse. Santiago and Officer Winslow were documenting everything, and I simply stood back and watched as they gathered samples of the candles and photographed every inch of the space that had been set up. I didn't want to interfere, and I really didn't have the energy to help, even if I could. I slid down the wall just inside the door and waited.

Once they were finished, Santiago suggested we talk outside in the sunshine, and I followed him slowly back into the light. This whole past week had been exhausting, but for some reason, finding this tribute depleted me. I don't know if it was that I was frustrated that someone was continuing to appropriate Celeste's image, if I was scared by the creepiness of the scene, or if I was angry that I couldn't actually do my job now. Maybe it was all three. But, whatever it was, the sight of all those candles and the photo had done me in. It had zapped me dry. I didn't even have the energy to smile at Santiago.

He reached into the front seat of his cruiser and handed me a Cheerwine. "Thought you could use this," he said as he pointed to a stump at the edge of the parking area.

I made my way over and sat down before popping open the soda and taking a sip. The sugar and the fizz zinged against my tongue, and I felt myself perk up just a tad. "Thanks," I said as I took another sip.

We sat silently for a few moments as I drank the soda, and then I finally said, "That was awful."

"Like a horror movie set. Was it worse for you than finding her body? Because it was worse for me." Santiago's words were quiet and timid.

I nodded. "Way worse, which I feel awful about. But yeah, way worse." I closed my eyes and tilted my head up and let the sunshine make my eyelids glow. "It was shocking and sad to find her body, but this felt ritualistic, not really about Celeste at all, you know?"

He sighed. "Yes, that's it exactly. The person who did this thinks they're paying tribute to her, but really, it's all about them."

We sat quietly for a moment, and then Santiago said, "I guess we know now why someone fired those blanks?"

I stared at him for a moment until I understood. "They needed chaos to steal the photograph."

He sighed and nodded. "It appears so."

Just then, Officer Winslow emerged from the front door of the warehouse, and Santiago caught her eye. "All clear?"

She nodded. "Doesn't look like anything else has been disturbed."

"Thanks," he said. "You'll get that evidence back and send it up to the lab?"

"Will do," she said as she climbed into her car and drove away.

I smiled. "That sounded very TV, that *sending things to the lab* stuff." I was feeling a bit better after the soda and after knowing that Santiago had been disturbed, too. I knew he'd seen a lot of things in his career, and if that whole setup had bothered him, well, then, at least I knew I wasn't a complete wuss.

"Well, I try to make my job seem extra glamorous to

impress you, you know?" He reached over and took my hand. "But we will send things to the lab, and since it's linked to a murder case, hopefully, they'll put it at the top of the pile."

I stood up. "Have time to take a walk?" I pointed toward the ravine behind the building. "Pretty wildflowers coming up down there."

He stood and wiped the dirt off his uniform pants and followed me back down the trail Sawyer and I had blazed. We walked in silence for quite a while before I said, "This is the person that posed her body, isn't it?"

Santiago audibly exhaled as he walked along behind me. "Yes, I expect so. We all knew that her body had been staged earlier, that she clearly hadn't been killed here, but this makes it clear that someone has a special reason for keeping her tied to this place."

"It's really disturbing, but does it maybe help eliminate people. I mean, I can't see Creedence or Stephen Davenport doing this. Can you?"

He shook his head. "Seems unlikely, but you know I can't rule anyone out yet."

"I know. This just feels too personal for them." I thought about what I'd just said. "I mean it seems less parental or something. I don't know."

"I see what you mean. With the candles and all, it feels more romantic."

I nodded. "Exactly." I shuddered. "You don't think Kyle . . ." I couldn't even finish my sentence.

"I doubt it. But again . . ." This time he didn't need to finish.

We walked quietly through the woods for a long time, but eventually, we knew we needed to get back. I had to sort through the items in the top two floors of the warehouse.

Santiago had said that would be fine but that I'd need to leave anything in the basement until later, which was totally cool with me.

I expected him to head out as soon as we climbed back up to the building, but instead, he radioed Officer Winslow, told her he was taking lunch, and then put his radio in the car. "Now, where do we start?" he said.

I smiled. I had been figuring I'd just make some more notes about the printing presses and measurements for the windows and doors I wanted to take, but if he was going to help, we might be able to load some of the smaller items into my car, including the boxes of books that were in the corner. "Let's start over here," I said, moving toward the presses.

The two of us were able to carry all three of the machines toward the door, and after laying a blanket into my car in case there was any ink still in the press, we put the smallest of the three into my hatch. I would be able to at least get the listing up online for that one item.

Then, we shifted all the boxes of books into my back seat, and I hoped I could find someone who would want to buy a lot of hand-printed books. It would be so much easier to sell them in one fell swoop, but if necessary, I could set up a sales listing somewhere and sell down the inventory over time.

Finally, we made our way to the top floor, and I scooped up all the cannery labels. I was just about to head down to my car with my last load when Santiago pointed toward a jumble of furniture in the corner and said, "Any of that worth anything to you?"

I set my armload at the top of the stairs and walked over to where he was pointing. I hadn't even noticed this assortment of chairs and tables when we were here before, probably because I was so excited about the historical labels. But now, I could see there were some really cool adjustable metal stools and some old metal tables in the mix, too. I didn't have room to take more today, but since Saul's crew was coming at one, I figured we could at least get these pieces out and downstairs to make things easier for them.

Slowly, we began to untangle the legs of the furniture, and soon we had a little array of metal pieces standing near the stairs for us to carry down. As we extricated the last table, I saw a glimmer of something in the corner. I thought it was probably an old can, since we'd found a couple of boxes of unused and lidless tomato cans amongst the furniture, but when I reached back to grab it, I saw the shine was coming from the buckle on an old journal.

It was a diary – a lot like the ones I had when I was a child with the strap and the clasp that anyone could open with a little effort, even if it was locked tight. The word "diary" was even written in gold letters on the front, just like mine from fifth grade.

I held the book up to show Santiago, and as I lifted it up toward my face so he could see it in the dim light from the dirty windows, I gasped. The name "Celeste Davenport" was pressed into the leather of the back cover in a child's handwriting.

"What is it, Paisley?" Santiago said as I scrambled around our furniture gambit to get to him.

"This was Celeste's diary – at least, I think it was," I said as I finally reached him. "See?" I turned the book over and showed him the back.

"Did you try to open it?" he asked.

I shook my head. "Do you want me to?"

He didn't hesitate. "Yes."

I flipped the small pink book back over and pushed the button that would spring the clasp up if it wasn't locked. Nothing happened. "It's locked. I can break it open, but . . ."

"Yeah, I'll need to take it back and get it logged before we do anything to it." He looked back toward the corner. "Show me exactly where you found it?"

I led him to the corner and pointed to the spot where the book had been lying. Clearly, it had been there awhile, given the rectangle of clean floor we could see where it had been.

Santiago knelt down and studied the corner carefully. Then, he took his pocketknife out, leaned forward, and pried a board away from the wall. A tumble of sparkly stickers, plastic jewelry, and nail polish poured onto the floor.

I stood back and stared. It looked like my fifth-grade fantasy – all that shiny stuff would have made eleven-year-old Paisley so happy. I'd never been a girl who wanted to wear the frilly things, and I don't think I'd ever put a bow in my hair. But sparkly stickers and glitter nail polish had been something I loved as a little girl, maybe because I liked the shine, maybe because I thought I should like all that stereotypically girly stuff.

I sat down on one of the stools and stared as Santiago snapped pictures with his phone. I knew instinctively that these were Celeste's things, but not the things of the twenty-eight-year-old woman we'd found downstairs. These were the things little Celeste had needed to keep hidden.

When Santiago finished recording the finds, we made our way back downstairs, and I called Saul to let him know that his crew wouldn't be needed today. "I can't explain, but I imagine Santiago can catch you up later."

"I'm sorry, Paisley," Saul said, "But I might just have

some good information that will help, from the get-together this morning. I'll share it with the good sheriff and let him tell you."

In the excitement of the morning, I had forgotten that Santiago and Saul had been scheduled to be at the VFW. My call had pulled Santiago away, but Saul must have stayed on to talk to the guys. "I could use some good news," I said quietly.

Saul cleared his throat on the other end of the line. "Couldn't we all." As always, he hung up without a good-bye, and I smiled. It was good some things never changed.

I needed to get on the road, but before I went, I wanted Santiago's take on what we'd found. "I know you can't tell me much, but—"

He interrupted me. "I expect that Celeste has been hiding out here for most of her life," he said. "You think the same thing, don't you?"

I nodded and had to swallow hard and look away to keep from crying. Just the thought of a child tucking away her little trinkets because it wasn't acceptable to others that she had them made me want to crawl in bed and sob. Instead, I said, "We have to figure out what happened to her, Santi."

He pulled me to him. "We will, Pais. We will. I think this will help, as hard as it is."

I stood up and wiped my eyes. "Do we need to put all these things back?" I gestured down toward my car.

"Nope, I'm coming to your house to go through them with you. Just let me take some photos of your car, and then wait for me before unloading, okay? I need to check in at the station, and I'll be right over."

"Okay," I said as I climbed into the driver's seat. "We'll see you at the house in a little while."

"Sawyer will be there?" Santiago said with a smile.

"Yeah, I need to see him so I'm going to ask Dad to bring him over."

"Good, I think I could use a look at his face, too." He looked away and took a deep breath before leaning in to kiss my cheek. "See you soon."

———

I caught Lucille up on the situation as I drove home, and she said she'd fill Dad in and that they'd both be over with Sawyer in about a half hour. "Sounds like this might call for a family gathering," she said.

As I hung up, I felt the tears come again and let myself cry it out for most of the ride. This situation was painful for everyone, but I just couldn't think about that little girl hiding away her nail polish. It broke my heart.

By the time I got home, my sadness had turned back into anger, and while sadness debilitates me, anger drives me. So by the time everyone arrived, I was ready to go. I had put out a folding table in the yard because I figured Sawyer would want to see me but knew that I needed to work. I set pens and note pads out, too, just in case there was anything we needed to record, and I made a pitcher of sweet tea.

Santiago smiled when he saw my setup, and when Dad arrived he patted my shoulder before they headed down the hill to Sawyer's playground. Lucille stopped, picked up a notepad, and said, "Where do you need me most?"

"If you could help us but also help with Sawyer if Dad needs you, that would be great." I felt a little bit like I needed to take charge of something here, and if Lucille was willing to take direction, I was going to give it.

"Absolutely," she said. "Just point me to where we begin."

"You need pictures of everything in my car?" I asked Santiago.

"Yep. Then we can unload." The three of us headed to the car, and Santiago snapped his pictures.

We unloaded the printing press first, and I took a few pictures myself before I asked Lucille to begin looking up similar machines and sales prices. She was a whiz with details, and I knew she'd find the information in no time.

Meanwhile, Santiago and I unloaded all the boxes of books, six in total, and set them up on the table. Sawyer stopped by, saw it was just "grown-up books," as he calls them, and returned to the swings, where Dad was waiting to push him as high as the trees.

I began by creating stacks of various titles as I sorted through each box. We found a couple of beautiful short-story collections and a wonderful cookbook for a local church, complete with hand-drawn illustrations for several of the dishes. There was even a beautifully printed program for a garden club tour back a few years. The cover featured bright circles of pink, yellow, and green, and the inside had full-cover prints of some of the oldest houses in Octonia. I knew immediately that Ms. Nicholas would like some copies for the historical society because of the object itself but also because of the descriptions of the houses that were included.

When we came to the box full of the lavender books filled with what I now knew to be Celeste's poetry, I paused, full of reverence and anxiety. These books held the thoughts she most wanted the world to know, and I wanted to treasure them in this simple form of ink on paper.

Lucille, Santiago, and I silently unboxed the five dozen

books and spread them gently on the table. Then, I opened the first page and read:

A four-petaled, blue flower
Is named purple by casual observers,
The man in the tweed newsboy hat,
The person in suspenders so red they make cardinals look pale.

But she calls herself Blue,
And she is right. Always.
Even when she grows on into green.

I sighed as I put the book back on the table. I knew four-petaled, blue flowers – the periwinkle at the edge of my yard – and I knew some people called it purple. I understood this, and so I understood, in some tiny way, Celeste.

"She wanted to be heard," Lucille said.

I sighed. "She did. And she will be." I looked down at the copies of the book on the table. "She will be."

———

We didn't find anything, beyond the copies of Celeste's books, that was relevant to her case, so we began to catalog what we had. Lucille had discovered that the model of press I had brought home was worth about four hundred dollars, and that was exciting news. I figured that if the books sold as a lot, I might make another two-fifty. So the prospect of having almost another month's mortgage payment lifted my spirits a bit.

But I wasn't going to include Celeste's books in that lot. I had the beginnings of another plan for those. I wasn't ready to talk about that yet. So I suggested we get pizza instead.

In my life experience, most people appreciate the simplicity and versatility of pizza. Lucille preferred a gluten-free crust, and my dad always needed soda to go with it. Mika was a no-meat-on-pizza woman, and I couldn't eat green peppers. Sawyer and Santiago would take anything that had cheese and tomato sauce. So I ordered our two pies, texted Mika to come over, and we all dined on one gluten-free cheese-and-mushroom pizza and one thin-crust sausage-and-pepperoni from the great little pizza shop in town. Add in a couple of beers and Sawyer being at his most winsome and silly, and we had a great night, despite the drama of the day.

Sawyer went down without a fuss since he was so tired from all the time with his grandparents, who always gladly helped him climb and jump off anything he desired, and Dad and Lucille went home to relax on their own couch. But Mika and Santiago stayed, and while I cleaned up the kitchen, they found more deadfall from the trees in the yard and built the second bonfire in the firepit in as many nights. It was lovely.

With a beer in hand, I took a seat by the fire and told Mika about the day, careful to only relay my own experience, not anything related to the investigation itself – not that Santiago had said anything today.

"You found her diary?" she asked. "Wow. I can't imagine what kind of things she wrote in a diary she thought she had to hide in a warehouse."

I pictured little-girl Celeste scribbling away in that dark corner, but then I realized that maybe it wasn't little-girl Celeste who had hidden those things there. Maybe she'd just stored them there when she was older. I knew I probably should wait to ask Santiago that question until later when we were alone, but the words tumbled out of my mouth before I could stop them. "Was it Celeste as a child that hid the diary? I know that's what we thought. But maybe she took it there when she was older, like after her parents kicked her out?"

Santiago gave me a sideways smile. "I thought the same thing this afternoon. She was definitely older when she hid them. So you don't have to worry that a little girl was tucked away up there in the dark."

I sighed. "How did you know that was what I was thinking?" I asked with a blush.

"You're a caring person with a big imagination, Paisley," he said quietly.

Mika giggled. "He does get you, friend."

My blush made my cheeks flame, so I swung the attention back to Celeste. "How did you know she was an adult?"

"Because she said so. The last entry in the journal says she's hiding it there for safekeeping so that her parents wouldn't destroy it." He sighed. "She wanted to keep it and the things with it to remind herself of how strong she was, she said."

Mika sniffled. "Oh man, the more I know about this woman the more I like her," she said as tears slid down her cheeks. "How could someone do this to her?"

I shook my head, but I had no answer to that really good question.

Santiago said, "I can't tell you specifics, of course, but if it helps, I think we did get a couple of good leads from Saul's work this morning."

"Well, good," I said. "Saul was at the VFW hall to talk to them about the dances that Celeste attended," I said to catch Mika up.

"Oh yeah? Cool." She knew that Santiago couldn't tell us anything that might compromise the investigation, but I knew that she was as eager as I was to hear anything he could share.

"It seems very likely, given what we learned today, that Celeste had been at the first dance that night as we thought she might have been," Santiago said.

I could see him wrestling with what he felt it was wise to say and what it wasn't. "Don't tell us anything you don't think we should know. Really. We're big girls and can handle waiting to hear." I meant what I said, and yet, I still wanted to know more.

"I won't, Pais," he said and reached over to take my hand.

I saw Mika smile and nod. "Okay, then tell us what you can," she said eagerly.

Santiago laughed. "The interesting thing is that the men said they remembered the dance she came to in particular for two reasons: one, it was the last dance she ever attended, and two, some guy was there making a big deal about her."

"What kind of big deal?" I asked.

"Talking her up to the men, telling them how amazing she was," Santiago said.

Mika pulled her legs under her. "That's weird. Sounds like he was trying to get her a date or something."

I nodded. "That is weird, especially since everyone there probably knew almost everyone else. Octonia isn't a big place."

Santiago grinned. "Believe me, I know."

"Could the men describe him?" I asked.

"Yeah, any distinctive tattoos?" Mika said.

I rolled my eyes, and Santiago shook his head. "Nothing

particularly notable. A younger, white guy people had seen around town but didn't really know. That's about it."

"Well, that doesn't really narrow it down," Mika said.

"No, it doesn't, but it's a new angle to consider in terms of her death." Santiago took a sip of his beer and stretched out his legs. I took that as the signal that this was all he felt comfortable sharing.

But that didn't mean that we couldn't speculate around him. "I don't think I'd like it if some guy was talking me up to other guys. It would feel sort of like he was selling me or something?"

"Right," Mika said, drawing out my line of thought. "Like he was pimping her out. Maybe he had something over her?"

We sat in silence for a bit before I said, "Is the coroner going to be able to pinpoint the exact day of death?" I suspected I knew the answer, but I thought I'd ask to be sure.

"No. We're as close as we're going to get to that date if we only have her bones to tell us information. But that time-line works out with what the men at the VFW hall told us," Santiago said.

"But if someone knew she was going to be out at a dance, then it would have been the perfect time to grab her and, well, kill her." It made me nauseated to even think of that, but it fit.

Mika sighed. "This is so sad." She looked at Santiago. "How do you do this all the time?"

Santiago sighed. "Fortunately, most of my job involves traffic tickets and people who forget it's not appropriate to pee in a parking lot. But these cases? They are wearing."

With that admission, I thought it best, for all of us maybe, if we changed the subject, so I told them about my vegetable garden plans and regaled them with the stories of how Sawyer had thought we would get magical peas four minutes after putting the seeds in the ground.

Mika shared a story of how, at age four, she had eaten all the bean seeds her father had planted and didn't confess that she had caused the strange bean shortage until two decades later, even though her father brought up the year the bean seeds were terrible every time they put in a garden.

Then, Santiago talked about how his mother had made him stand in the garden every morning to watch for shoots coming through the soil. "It was the greatest thing when I saw one. I always thought it had happened while I was watching."

I thought about that. "Well, it has to happen sometime, right? Why not while you were watching?" I asked.

"Fair question," he said. "But one morning, I ran into the house to tell Mama that all the corn had come up while I stood there." He paused and cleared his throat. "She called me her Magic Mijo from then on. It's still my family nickname."

I squeezed his hand and then stood up. "Well, mis amigos, it's time for me to go to bed."

Mika hugged me and then headed straight to her car, and I once again thought how lucky I was to have a friend who understood just what I needed and wasn't offended or hurt when it wasn't time with her.

I pulled Santiago close. "I'd love to meet your mother someday. She sounds amazing."

"She is, and you will." He looked at me. "You and Sawyer, but only when you're ready, okay?"

"Okay," I said, and kissed him.

I checked on Sawyer, who was splayed across my bed and snoring, and then made a cup of tea. I was a little too keyed up to sleep just yet, and my cross-stitch was calling my name. I sat down and threaded my needle with an emerald-green thread that was going to be, aptly, a spool of thread in the piece and began to sew.

As I stitched, I realized something was working itself out in the back of my mind. Something about what Santiago said about the garden and watching for the sprouts that he always thought he caught sight of when one came up.

I put the needle in and pulled the thread up, and then as I plunged it back through the fabric, a question rose up in my mind. What if that's what happened with Celeste? What if someone had been watching her, saw her at the dance, and realized it was the perfect chance to grab her? Someone might have seen an opportunity and taken it.

The more I sewed and pondered, the more that seemed likely. But that would have meant someone had to be stalking Celeste and waiting, and that felt even more horrible than just someone acting on an opportunity.

Still, I kept coming back to the question of why. A lot of people bore a lot of hate toward trans people, so that was definitely a possibility. But what if hate had nothing to do with it? Jealousy? Anger? Desperation?

As I put the final stitches in the spool of thread, I wondered, for the first time, who Celeste had dated and who she had not. A jilted lover or would-be lover might have a lot of reasons to kill a beautiful young woman. And I knew just who to ask.

Chapter Eleven

The next morning, Sawyer and I headed down to the historical society. I wanted to give Ms. Nicholas those garden club programs, and I was hoping to catch Trevor on hand. If anyone knew who the guy might have been at the dance or who might have been interested in Celeste, it was him. The best friend always knew all that stuff.

When we arrived, Saw and I settled into the research room with crayons, blank paper, and not a historical document in sight. That boy didn't honor paper as a prime coloring spot, but I was certain that if I put out a one-of-a-kind letter, he'd want to scribble on it first thing. Ms. Nicholas had welcomed us warmly and was fetching both of us a cup of tea, mine hot and Sawyer's not. He'd taken to really liking tea, as long as it was room temperature, sweet, and milky. I could relate to two of the three.

For my part, I'd brought along one of Lucille's famous pineapple upside-down cakes on the premise that it was totally fitting for breakfast. I figured a thank-you was in order for all Ms. Nicholas had done for me and Santiago, and for hosting Celeste's memorial. Plus, it gave me an excuse to eat cake for breakfast.

Ms. Nicholas returned with three mugs of mint tea and set one before each of us. I put a small towel out under Sawyer's and turned on his videos with the hopes that crayons, tea, and *Brain Candy* would buy me a few minutes.

"Thank you so much for everything you did this weekend," I said when Ms. Nicholas sat down across from us. "That was a terribly kind gift you gave Celeste."

Ms. Nicholas nodded. "I was glad to do it, for Trevor mostly. He's been so distraught since they" – she looked up at me quickly – "since you found her body. It must have been like losing her all over again. He was just so upset."

"I can't even imagine. Maybe they can both have peace now." I sighed and took a sip of my tea before asking my question. "Actually, I was hoping Trevor might be here. I wanted to ask him something about Celeste."

I knew I was treading a thin line here and that I might just be walking right into actual police investigation work, but I had a sense that Trevor might open up to me more than to Santiago. If that happened, I'd encourage him to tell the police what he knew, and I'd tell Santiago myself, too.

"Oh, well, he was due to be here about a half hour ago." She looked down at her watch. "Let me give him a call." She stepped outside the room, and I could hear her leaving what was obviously a message. When she came back in, she looked worried. "It isn't like Trevor to be late – and he didn't pick up his phone."

"Did you try texting him?" I said. "Sometimes people don't answer a call but will a text." I knew that was true for me, at least.

Ms. Nicholas pursed her lips, but she sent off a quick

message. When no reply came immediately, she put her phone down on the table. "Maybe he'll be here soon," she said half-heartedly.

"Maybe. In the meantime, let's have some cake." At the magic word, Sawyer's head popped up, and I cut him a small slice of sweet, gooey goodness before serving Ms. Nicholas and me much more hefty pieces. "I also brought you something."

I pulled the garden club brochures out of my satchel and slid them across the table. Ms. Nicholas's face lit up, and she carefully opened and studied each page. "These are gorgeous, and we don't have anything like them. Can I ask where they came from?"

I told her about the boxes of product in the warehouse and how delighted I was to find these because they were so beautiful and because I knew she'd love them.

"I do love them, but these are over-the-top as advertising material, even for the garden club." She kept turning the brochure over again and again.

"I thought so, too. Don't they usually just print a sort of mini-magazine on really thin paper?" I was remembering an incident with last year's brochure and spilled apple juice.

"Right. They want it to show color, for good reason, but they don't want all their proceeds to go to printing." She studied the back of the brochure. "I wonder what changed things that year."

I picked up the other copy and began reading it. On the third page, I came to a blinding halt. "Oh no," I said, realizing I should have read the brochure instead of just admiring it.

Ms. Nicholas looked at me. "Are you okay? Whatever is the matter?"

I so wanted to tell her, but this was the kind of thing

Santiago needed to hear firsthand. "I'm sorry, Ms. Nicholas. Do you mind if I step out and make a quick phone call? It's really important."

She smiled and nodded. "I'll keep Sawyer busy if he needs me." She watched me as I left, and I knew I needed to explain, but first, I needed Santiago to hear this.

He answered his cell on the first ring. "Good morning, Sunshine," he said. "I would love for this to be a quick perk in my Monday morning, but since you don't usually opt to use the phone, especially when Little Man is around, I suspect this isn't just a social call."

"Sadly, it's not, but I like that you know that about me," I said with a blush. "I'm at the historical society. I just read something I think you need to see. Can you come over?"

I could hear him stand up and move toward the door. "Paperwork can wait. I'll be there in five minutes."

When I went back inside the museum house, Ms. Nicholas had pulled her chair over next to Sawyer, and he was explaining what the pandas and rabbits on *BabyBus* were doing. It was something involving a fire, a smoke detector, and the woods.

I took the minute to review the brochure again, just to be sure I was putting everything together correctly while also hoping I'd misread. Sadly, I was correct, and now, Santiago's case was probably going to get even more complicated. And ugly. Quite ugly.

I sat back down at the table near Sawyer and tried to pay attention to his videos, but it was hopeless. I kept thinking about Celeste's face smiling in that photograph, about how it had been so joyous at her memorial and then how creepy it had seemed at the warehouse. I would be fine to never see that photo again.

When Santiago came in, Ms. Nicholas stood and said,

"Sawyer, I wonder if you could help me pick some daffodils for the table here." She took a pair of garden clippers from the top of a file cabinet. "I'll even help you use these." She gave me a quick glance, and I nodded. Saw did fine with supervised use of scissors and the like.

"Thanks, Ms. Nicholas," I said. "We won't be but a minute."

She smiled and then guided Sawyer out the front door with a gentle hand on the back of his head.

Santiago sat down next to me, and even though he smiled, I could see how very weary he looked. His skin was a little sallow, and I wondered how much sleep he was getting. "I'm sorry to call you out, but I knew you'd want to see this. And with Sawyer with me . . ."

He put his hand on mine. "I'm happy to be here, and yeah, it's best to not bring Sawyer to the police station unannounced. This morning, we had a couple of guys pretty riled up because they'd been picked up for drunk and disorderly last night."

I sighed, glad he understood. I handed him the brochure and pointed to the words that had stopped me cold. "This year's Octonia Garden Club Tour chair is Creedence Davenport." The rest of the paragraph went on to describe how Mrs. Davenport was eager to make this year's tour the best ever, and she was glad to have "the support of her *entire* family in this important work for the community."

Santiago sat back and stared at the booklet. "And Celeste printed these." His words were a statement, not a question.

I nodded. "Looks like she went all out to produce something that would make her mother proud." The idea of that effort clashed so fully with the ugliness I had seen from Mrs.

Davenport on Saturday, and I felt my anger rising again. "Clearly, her mother didn't appreciate her efforts."

He set the program back on the table. "Looks like I need to talk to some of the women from the garden club and learn a bit more about what happened that year." He leaned his head back and looked at the ceiling. "The tour usually takes place in May, right?"

I thought about the cute little yard signs that the houses on the tour put up each year and could remember them in front of lush green forsythia bushes and surrounded by the tall spires of blue salvia or against the bursting blooms of peonies. "Yeah, that sounds right," I said. I considered what I knew of the club and offered a thought. "Dad has given several talks to the club over the years. Maybe take him with you?"

"Actually, I'm wondering if you might be willing to go – with your dad if you want – to talk to them. You know a lot about plants, and you could use these brochures as a premise to go to their next meeting." He paused and looked at me. "I don't like to involve you, you know that, but I think they may talk more freely with you than with me."

He had a point, and Dad would be a welcome guest, even with me in tow, because they loved to ply him for gardening advice and try to get him to put his house on the tour, something he had staunchly refused for more than three decades. "They just want pretty flowers, and they like to coach me on what I should plant. I don't need their input," he grumbled every year.

"Okay, I'll do it. But you really are the better plant expert, you know?" I smiled at him as I took out my phone. "Let me see when their next meeting is." I searched for the club online. Their very simple but very professional website came up, and I groaned. "Their next meeting is in two hours."

I looked out at the yard, where Sawyer was very carefully cutting flowers as Ms. Nicholas guided his hands. "I have Sawyer, and I don't think I can take him with me. Maybe Lucille—"

Santiago cut me off. "Let me call Winslow and see what the situation is at the station. If the two rowdy guys have cleared out, I can take him with me, and we can play in the jail cell and test out the radios. Sound okay?"

I smiled. "Yes, he would love that." I stood and headed toward the front of the building while I called Dad. Fortunately, Lucille answered his phone and said, without hesitation, that he'd meet me at the Taylor House, the location for today's meeting, at eleven forty-five, and she'd call the president of the club, an old friend of hers, and let her know we were coming to talk about a beautiful old program that I had located. She offered to watch Sawyer, too, but I let him know he already had a date with a jail cell. She loved that idea.

"Thanks, Lucille," I said as I hung up and walked over to see the massive handful of daffodils my son had picked.

"These are for you," he said as he held them up to me. "I picked them myself."

I smiled and took the flowers. "Thank you, Love Bug." I selected one stem and put it into the ponytail at the back of my head. "I'll keep this one, but the rest would look pretty inside, don't you think?"

"Help me find the right vase and pour the water," Ms. Nicholas said as we moved toward the door and Sawyer ran ahead. "Everything okay?"

"Yes," I looked at Santiago, who was waiting by the door when we came in. "I'll be right back, Ms. Nicholas."

As she followed Sawyer into the kitchen, I asked Santiago if I could tell her what we'd found. "I feel weird because she was just sitting here, and now I'm keeping this secret, and we're in her space, and she's helping with Sawyer—"

He put a hand on my arm. "Sure, do tell her. I'm not in the business of secrets, just good police work."

I smiled and made my way to the kitchen, where Sawyer was very carefully filling a vase imprinted with the pattern of a beehive, a gift I'd given Ms. Nicholas a few weeks earlier to say thank you for all her help. I'd found it in an old barn, and I knew nothing about it except that it was lovely.

As Sawyer filled the vase and then emptied it again and again, I told Ms. Nicholas about the brochure and who had been chairperson of the tour that year and said that we now needed to explore how this affected the case. I didn't say more about the specifics because of the toddler's presence, but I figured she'd understand.

"I see. Shall I pull our garden club file as well?" she asked with a smile.

I grinned. "Of course you have a garden club file. I should have known. Yes, please," I said, and moved toward the sink to take over supervising. At this rate, Sawyer was going to drain the society's well, so it looked like it was time to do a little game of flower arranging instead.

We carried the blooms and the full vase to a small table in the foyer of the building. I let Sawyer slide each stem into the water, and then he moved them around until he was satisfied. "It's perfect," he said.

Santiago and I were admiring his very good arrangement when the front door of the society opened and Trevor wandered in. He looked rough – his clothes were disheveled, and he hadn't shaved in a couple of days. When he turned to look at us, I could see that his eyes were blood-shot, and he smelled strongly of alcohol.

Quickly but casually, Santiago stepped between Trevor and Sawyer and me, and I told my son we were going to go upstairs and explore, hoping that Ms. Nicholas wouldn't mind, given the situation.

She appeared just as we began to climb the stairs oppo-site the research room, took one look at Trevor, and gave me a firm nod. I bustled Sawyer the rest of the way up, and we spent the next few minutes looking at the racks of old clothing that people had donated over the years and that the society used for tours and such. My son took a particular liking to a tricornered hat, and I made a mental note to pick up a toy one and some books about nineteenth-century Virginia for him. My little guy wasn't much of a reader, but he did like knowing things, just like his mama.

Right then, his mama was dying to know what was happening downstairs, but I realized that the presence of a busy young body probably wasn't the best idea, for the conversation or for my son. Sawyer needed to experience the realities of the world, but maybe not that up close and personal. Santiago would fill me in later, I was sure.

We were just about to lace up some Victorian booties when I heard footsteps on the stairs and saw Santiago's face peek around the doorframe. "What is happening up here?" he boomed in mock seriousness.

Saw's face lit up. "I playing dress-up," he said. Then he pulled a long velvet coat off a hanger and handed it to Santiago. To his credit, the sheriff didn't even hesitate in putting it on, and for a few minutes, he and Sawyer were "fancy men," walking around in old-town Octonia. They bought fruit from a street market, picked up some nails from the mercantile, and cleaned up after a horse – that was Sawyer's favorite part. I couldn't decide if I was more impressed by how well Santiago imagined with my son or with his knowledge of history. I decided it was a tie.

Eventually, Santiago let it slip that he might need some help at the police station because the jail cell needed testing, and Sawyer jumped up and said, "Mama, I help Santi."

I smiled and said I thought that was a very good idea. "Maybe you can go with Santiago, and I'll go to a meeting. How does that sound?"

"That sound good," Sawyer said and then took my hand and Santiago's hand to walk down the very narrow staircase. It was an awkward but incredibly sweet descent.

Trevor had apparently gone on his way, and I was glad. I had wanted to talk to him, but clearly, I needed to wait for another time. He had been in no state for me to ask him questions.

Santiago and Sawyer said goodbye, and I watched Sawyer skip hand in hand down the sidewalk with this man who understood how to love him so well. Then, I turned toward Ms. Nicholas and gave her a tight hug. "Thank you. Are you okay?"

She hugged me back and then began to arrange the papers on the table beside the daffodils. "I am, but Trevor" – she looked up at me – "is most certainly not."

Her face was creased with worry, and I wanted to hug her again. I knew, though, that sometimes when one is trying to keep oneself under control, kindness can let that control slip. Ms. Nicholas was at work, and crying at work was not ideal. "Yeah, he didn't look well. You'll check on him later?"

"I will. I thought I'd take him some soup later. Should I tell him you want to speak with him? That is, if he looks up to it?" Her gaze was steady and true.

"Actually, I think I'll let Santiago talk to him. I expect they discussed that?" I hoped they'd discussed that.

Ms. Nicholas nodded. "Our sheriff is a good man, both caring and professional. He gave Trevor space but also made it clear that they would need to have a further conversation, and soon."

"Yeah." I pointed back toward the research room. "Do keep that brochure, and when I can, I'll bring you another copy to replace the one that I need for today when I come to look at that garden club file." I held up the booklet before sliding it into my bag.

"Thank you," she said. "Now, don't you have a garden club meeting to get to?"

I slipped my phone out of my pocket. Ten thirty. I had just enough time to get home, change clothes, and make the thirty-minute ride to the meeting. Jeans were not going to cut it for the garden club ladies.

Right at eleven forty-five, I pulled up in front of the Taylor House. Despite the terrible reason for us to come to the meeting and my growing anxiety about sitting in the same room with Creedence Davenport after our encounter on Saturday, I was quite excited to see the inside of this old house. A quick search of the National Historic Registry told me the house had been built in about 1830 by one of Octonia's wealthiest families, the Taylors. They had made their money, as had most of the wealthy planters in this area, by farming with enslaved labor. While I was eager to see the inside of the house because I loved all historic buildings, I was also hoping the meeting would include a "garden" tour so I could see if any of the outbuildings were where those enslaved people had worked and lived. I never had much interest in the owners of these places, but I was captivated by the strength and resilience of the people who had labored here.

Dad was waiting in his truck when I arrived, and so I parked in the grass next to him. I imagined that we were violating all kinds of etiquette by parking so willy-nilly on the lawn, but I didn't really care. Country people parked anywhere the ground was dry, and I wasn't about to spend an extra half hour here while people moved their cars off the circular drive just so I could get out.

"So why am I here?" Dad grumbled as we walked toward the front of the house.

I gave him the quick rundown on the brochure and what Santiago and I needed to know about Mrs. Davenport that year. "I just hope some of these women remember," I said.

Dad laughed. "Have you met the women of the garden club? These women remember everything. Don't slight them, Paisley. They never forget." He was still smiling, but I heard the warning in his words.

As we approached the tall climb of steps to the front portico, we noticed a small lawn sign that read "Garden Club" and pointed around the side of the house. We walked to the right and passed by windows with wooden bars on them, a feature I had never seen on a plantation house before, and then past a small building that might have been a kitchen or something like a workspace for weavers or cobblers. The smokehouse was next, and I hoped that before we left, I might be able to put my head inside and smell the centuries of fires that had burned there.

As we reached the back of the house, I could see a circle of chairs beneath the arms of a huge pin oak, and beyond that, a small wooden structure sat at the edge of the historic lawn. I knew just by looking it was a slave quarter, and again, I hoped I could look inside.

Now though, I had to focus, so I put on my best smile, wiped my hand on the side of my black dress pants, and slipped my right arm through Dad's. He would need me to help him hear, and I needed him to help keep me cordial.

We spent the next few minutes "meeting and greeting," and not for the first time, I was surprised by not only how many people my dad knew well but by how well he could schmooze when he wanted to. He had a lifetime of back-story with most of these women, and he pulled out spouses and children's names like he was reading from a cheat sheet. And they loved his attention. I felt a little brilliant at the idea of inviting him.

By the time the meeting started, Dad had agreed to talk for five minutes about his strategy for planting in shade, and I had been given another slot of time to ask about the history of the club and, in particular, the brochure I had discovered.

While the club did its usual business of approving minutes and reporting the treasury – these women had some moolah for flowers – I scrambled to pull together a series of questions that would camouflage what I really wanted to know while still giving me crucial information. I was feeling flustered, and my rising discombobulation wasn't helped by the icy glares that Mrs. Davenport kept throwing me across the circle.

I nodded. "Hermie?"

"Short for Hermione." He smiled. "Her parents were very interested in Greek history."

"So not Harry Potter then?" I teased.

He rolled his eyes and climbed the ladder to the loft.

Chapter Twelve

When I got to the station to pick up Sawyer, I found him sleeping peacefully in the jail cell. Officer Winslow smiled and said, "He insisted. Said he was going to jail for hitting his Baba."

I laughed. "He plays that way a lot, but now we're going to have to up our game. Not sure the pantry is going to stand up as a jail against an actual cell." I watched my son for a moment to see. "Officer Winslow, do you mind letting me know when he wakes up? I need to talk to Santiago."

"Of course. It's kind of soothing to hear his little breaths over there," she said. "And please, call me Savannah. I think we're past the need for formalities."

"Savannah, then. Thanks." I smiled as I passed her and decided I would ask Lucille if she could make her some of her famous shortbread. This woman had helped me more times than I could count, and I owed her. Someday I'd be able to bake my own thank-yous, but until tiny hands let me produce more than very simple drop cookies, Lucille was happy to help.

I knocked on the door of Santiago's office, and he invited me in with a hearty "welcome."

"Did you know it was me?" I asked when I came in. "That was a warm welcome for someone with bad news."

He smiled, walked over, and closed the door behind me. "Winslow texted that you were here, so I assumed." He gave me a quick hug and returned behind his desk.

I sat down across from him and said, "I wanted to tell you about the garden club meeting while it was fresh in my mind."

"Great," he said, "and I have a couple of updates for you, too."

"I get updates now," I said with a twinkle in my eye.

"You do . . . a perk of the relationship." He winked. "You first."

I told him about the meeting, about how Celeste had asked Robard to print the materials for free, and about the hostility amongst the group members. "I think Mrs. Davenport might have overestimated the value of prejudice in her election run."

"Oh, I hope you're right," he said. "And that's good info, and it makes sense with what Robard told me this morning."

I sat up straighter. "You talked to him?"

"He came in this morning," he said. "He'd heard about the shrine and was really upset. Said he couldn't believe someone would have the audacity to break in again. He's having the locks changed."

I thought about that a minute. "What did you think of his reaction?" I wondered if this was a case of protesting too much or genuine concern. "I mean, the building is about to be torn down, so changing the locks seems like, well, a little extreme."

"That was my first take, too, but then he mentioned the chance that someone could get really hurt and how you still needed to get into your salvage job." He puffed out a breath. "I think he was sincere."

I nodded. "Okay, that's good to hear because I was a bit suspicious . . ." I decided not to finish my thought.

"Totally understood. But maybe it will help to hear what Trevor said this morning?" He raised an eyebrow.

"I didn't want to ask, but is he okay?" I hadn't yet figured out how to tell Santiago that I had some questions for Trevor myself but thought maybe now I wouldn't have to.

"He went on quite a bender after the service, it seems. Said he started drinking that afternoon and just woke up when Ms. Nicholas called him this morning." He rubbed his face. "The kid is in a bad place."

"And you're concerned that maybe it's not just grief making him so upset?" I asked.

"Exactly. Grief can do that to a person. Believe me, I've seen it." He studied his hands. "Even years later, people can still be totally upended by a memory."

"Much less an entire service," I added.

He nodded. "But there was something about what Trevor said that made me concerned. Do me a favor and steer clear of him for a bit, okay?"

I studied his face and decided I needed to share what I'd wanted to know from Trevor. "Okay, I will. But I was wondering something and had thought to ask him."

Santiago smiled. "What were you wondering?"

"That shrine – it really seemed like a tribute, something put together by someone who loved Celeste." I paused. "Or at least thought they did. I wondered if Trevor might know who that someone was."

"Or if Trevor was that someone?" Santiago said.

"Yeah, now that you tell me this, that did occur to me." I sighed. "I was going to ask him about it this morning at the historical society."

Santiago tilted his head. "Because?"

"I thought he might talk to me more than he would you, just like with the garden club." I was stretching to justify my actions, and I knew it.

Santiago got up and came around the desk. "I see what you mean, but let's not get you in over your head, okay?" He took my hand in his. "I don't want to lose you, and Sawyer can't."

I nodded. He was right. "No more investigating for me." I pulled his hand into my lap. "But can I get busy doing my job?"

"You are free to gather the rest of the items from the warehouse. You'll let Saul know?"

"I will," I said as I stood and pulled him up with me. "Now, I need to go sit with my son in jail."

He smiled. "Sounds like a plan," he said as he pulled me close.

———

While Sawyer snoozed away on the cot, I sat on the chair Savannah had given me and called Saul. Normally, I would text in this situation – or any other – but Saul did not answer texts. Considered them rude, in fact. It was about time for Sawyer to wake up anyway, so I risked the conversation.

"Hi, Saul. I have good news," I said when he answered.

"You've decided to take up confectionary?" He had a sweet tooth that should have rotted out twenty years ago.

"Alas, that's my retirement plan, so I hope you make it." It was part of my deal with Saul – I'd let him make the occasional mild sexist comment with only an eye roll in response, and I got to call him old. It worked for us.

He laughed. "So the real news?"

I told him we were cleared to begin on the warehouse, and he said his crew could be there at three if that suited me.

I pulled my phone away from my ear and saw it was two-thirty. "Okay. I may be a minute late. I have Sawyer" – I looked down to see my son beginning his very languorous wake-up process – "and he's just waking up."

"No problem. We'll start with the big stuff and wait for you on directions for everything else." He hung up.

I smiled down at the phone and then pulled a warm, fluffy-headed toddler into my lap for a quick snuggle. He rested against me until I said, "Want to go play in a big, empty, dirty building?" Then, he was up and moving fast. The key word was "dirty," I was sure.

―――――――

By the time we arrived at the warehouse at just after three, the crew had pulled the other two printing presses out and was bringing the canning machine up from the basement. Saul led me inside to the piles they'd made of everything else – a few more boxes of letterpress books, a really interesting collection of glass bottles, and a few dozen windows with most of their panes intact. "Looks like we could build a couple of greenhouses to sell, from these and the window wall at the back," I said as I approved the loading of everything into the truck.

"Agreed." He took another look around and said, "I

think that's everything that's not attached. We'll start on the building itself tomorrow."

I nodded. "Sounds good." I took a quick look through the door to see that Sawyer was safely out of the way of all the moving equipment as he watched the truck lift with fascination before I said, "Nothing amiss downstairs, right?"

"Nope, nothing."

I sighed. "Good. That was just terrifying."

"I bet it was," a deep voice said from the doorway behind me. "That's why I've been sleeping here with some floodlights on. Figured that would deter the shrine maker."

Robard Greene stood in the doorway, and his frame blocked most of the light. I don't know if it was my uneasiness in the building because of my last two visits, my suspicions of him directly, or just motherly instinct, but I didn't like that he was between me and my son. "Good to see you, Mr. Greene." I stepped forward to him, and he moved out of the way.

"Your son is a natural operator, Paisley," he said with a laugh.

Saul came out from behind me and said, "Well, clearly, I'll need him to start on the crew as soon as he can get a work permit. Or if you're up for it, I can pay him under the table to run the lift."

I rolled my eyes at the two men but smiled myself when I saw my toddler standing with one of the men who was letting him operate the lift controls. He was following directions from the crew as they needed him to raise and lower the lift. He was in his version of heaven. "You guys okay with that?" I asked one of the men.

"Are you kidding? It frees up a man to carry things," the guy answered. "We'll keep an eye on him if you want."

I glanced over at Saul. "The guys all have kids, too. He'll be okay for a few minutes."

Sawyer wasn't paying a bit of attention to me, so I suggested we take a look at the basement, "just to double-check to be sure we didn't miss anything." Really, I wanted to watch Robard's reaction when we went down. I didn't know what I was watching for exactly, but I figured if he was hesitant or over-eager, it might mean something.

"Sure," Robard said. "Looks to me like you got it all, but always good to double-check."

I sighed. He clearly wasn't nervous about going down. The man had slept here the past two nights, though, so maybe we were looking at too much ease.

The three of us made our way down the stairs inside, but when we got to the bottom and turned into the room, all of us stopped and looked at the elevator shaft. It was empty, except for the puddles of dried white wax on the floor. Santiago and Savannah had taken everything out. But I could still envision the candles and remember Celeste's photo.

"I haven't been able to come down here on my own," Robard said. "Just too disturbing."

I sighed. "Yeah, it was the creepiest thing I'd ever seen."

Saul cleared his throat. "We'll get to work taking the building down tomorrow, Robard. Take away the temptation for whoever has done this."

Robard nodded. "I'd appreciate that. I had really hoped to remember Celeste in this place with fondness, but now . . ." He paused and turned toward the door. "Now, it just needs to be gone."

After I pried Sawyer's tiny fingers from the lever of the truck lift, he and I went home and played all afternoon. I threw myself into the travels of tiny concrete mixers and forklifts and tried to work all my shoulder muscles while he was on the swing, anything I could do to stop my mind from running again and again over who might have killed Celeste and why. By the time Sawyer and I lay down to listen to some David Gray, a favorite singer of his and the one he called "Bob," I was so exhausted I could have gone to sleep right then and there.

But once he dozed off, I got up, made some tea, and took out my cross-stitch. I needed to slow down my brain, so I cued up my new streaming channel trial and put on *The Real World Homecoming*. Once I had gotten over the fact that these folks were reuniting after thirty years – and realized just what that meant for my own age – I was really looking forward to seeing what I remembered about the characters and to thinking about how reality television had changed over three decades. At least that's what I told myself as I picked up my sewing and decided to work on another billow of curtain at one side of the piece.

A couple of hours and a full curtain of stitches later, my phone vibrated, and I smiled to see Santiago's name there: *Got time for a call?* he asked.

I stepped into the kitchen so that my voice wouldn't wake Sawyer and smiled again when he answered. I was clearly smitten, and now, I didn't even care. "This is a nice surprise."

He laughed. "I had hoped to make it over, but I'm kind of buried. I needed your take on something, though. Savannah and I concur on the situation, but she suggested you might have a helpful perspective."

"As a historian?'"

"Actually, as a mom," he said, and his voice grew more serious. "Trevor explained this morning that Mrs. Davenport threatened him just after the memorial service, told him that if he continued this nonsense about burying Celeste under that name she would ruin him."

I wanted to scoff about the old-fashioned threat, but given what I'd seen of the Davenports, I figured it might be more than a threat. "Oh, how awful. No wonder he was so upset. She's a very intimidating person to anyone, but I'd think especially to Trevor since he knew what she'd done to her own daughter."

"That's exactly the reason we thought you might be able to help." He sighed. "Putting aside the real reasons Creedence Davenport wants to lie about Celeste's identity, what would you do if you thought someone was a danger to Sawyer or his reputation?"

I sat down at the barstool by the counter and said, without pause, "Anything I could." I took a breath, stifled back my sob, and said, "Especially if he was already dead." Tears were streaming down my face. I hated thinking about these things, but I knew Santiago needed my insight here.

His voice grew soft on the line. "I'm sorry, Paisley. We didn't realize how painful it would be to even think that way. I guess that's why we needed to ask you to do it."

"It's okay," I said, my voice thick with tears. "I want to help, and I'll go upstairs in a bit and hug him close. It's alright. Keep going."

"You sure?"

I cleared my throat. "Yes, go on."

"Why did you say you'd do anything especially if he was dead?" I could hear the strain as he said the words, too.

"Because I take very seriously my role as Sawyer's guide, and I am very conscientious about doing anything he might then do after he saw me do it. But if he was already gone, well, then I'd have far fewer reasons to hold back than I would if he was alive." I swallowed hard and thought about Mrs. Davenport again. "Are you thinking she's trying to protect Celeste?" I didn't want to believe that given how awful she'd been to her own daughter, but I could see it, in a sick, hateful kind of way.

"Yeah, we're wondering if she might have built that shrine in the last place her child lay to pay some sort of last respects to her." He paused. "But that just doesn't fit, does it? She wouldn't have used that picture of Celeste."

"No, she wouldn't have," I said. "That wasn't her doing, and I don't think she put her body there either. If she had, she would have dressed her as a man, don't you think?"

Santiago moaned. "Yes, well, there goes that theory. She's clearly just threatening people to get her own way," he said.

"Well, I don't know about that." His original theory had merit, but it just didn't get us closer to answers about her death. "She may still be threatening people she thinks are doing her daughter harm. Maybe she knows something you need to know?" I knew he wasn't going to like that idea, but now that we were talking about this, I thought it might be worthwhile to ask her.

"I'm going to have to talk to her again, aren't I?" A rustling on his end of the line made me think he had just dropped onto a couch or bed.

"I'm sorry." I sighed. "Want me to go with you?"

"No, this is my burden to bear, but thanks. Talk to you tomorrow?"

"Definitely," I said before saying goodbye and hanging up. I didn't envy him at all as I climbed the stairs and got into bed next to my sleeping toddler. I fell asleep with my cheek against his.

Chapter Thirteen

I woke up the next morning with not only my drool but Sawyer's on my cheek, but it was worth it because we had both slept soundly all night long. I couldn't remember the last time that had happened, and it was glorious.

Even Saw must have been feeling good because he ate and dressed without complaint. He was excited to go spend the day with his Baba and Boppy. I had decided, despite Saul assuring me I didn't need to be on-site for this demo, that I wanted to be there, mostly to honor Celeste's memory, but also because I wanted to learn how to do this part of my job better. Saul was always happy to help, and I was grateful. This business was mine, though, and I was determined to learn how to do all of it – well, except for running the equipment. I'd let Saul's crew do that until Sawyer could.

I didn't even get out of the car at Dad's house because Lucille met us at the curb and scooped Sawyer up with a hug and a promise of trampoline time with her. She was a far better person than I was because I *never* agreed to get on that bone-jarring thing. I waved and pulled out, thankful for a bit of quiet time to myself.

I kept thinking about what Santiago had suggested about Mrs. Davenport wanting to protect Celeste, and the more I thought, the more I realized that this was exactly what she was doing. Of course, it wasn't a disinterested protection. Mrs. Davenport clearly thought she had something to gain, too. But the irony was that she was only hurting her daughter and herself by this hateful behavior.

Sadly, life had taught me too well that you can't make someone do better or learn. They have to choose that for themselves. But if I'd thought I could get her to stop, I would have tried. I just knew it would be futile.

When I got to the warehouse, I checked my emails and saw one from Trevor. He wanted to know if I'd like to come to a small graveside ceremony for Celeste tomorrow. "Just for friends and family, but we'd like to have you there. Sawyer, too," he said.

I replied immediately that I'd be honored. I wanted to ask him how he was, but I figured that was none of my business and something he'd share with me if and when he wanted, but probably not via text.

As I put my phone back in my pocket, I reminded myself to ask Santiago how Trevor had pulled off being able to bury Celeste after all. That was such a great bit of news to start the day. Then, I started thinking about whether Sawyer should come and if so, how I would talk with him about a funeral. I didn't get far down that train of thought though because a huge forklift just barely avoided taking off the door of my car. I jumped out and was ready to shout when I saw Saul's grinning face in the cab. "Gotcha," he said before climbing down. "Those smartphones will be the end of all of us."

I rolled my eyes and walked over, sliding my hard hat on as I went. "I just got a message from Trevor. They're holding a small graveside service for Celeste on Thursday."

He nodded. "They are."

"You were invited, too?"

"Something like that." He turned toward the building. "As always, we'll start with the roof." His switch to demo talk told me this conversation was over, and he was ready to get to work. The crew gathered around, and Saul gave them their marching orders. Soon, they were off and so was the roof. Next, they took down the rafters and then pulled down the upper story walls. Nothing much to salvage there – too much water damage.

But the floorboards and beams under that second story were in good shape, and the crew made quick work of stacking the beams on the back of the tractor trailer and setting the boards aside to be loaded later.

Within two hours, they had moved on to the window wall at the back of the building. Once I saw that was well in hand, I decided to take a walk. I had been trying to look nonchalant and casual because I hated when other people watched me work and thought the crew might feel the same. But I was tired of scrolling Facebook, and I could not beat my level on my current game obsession.

The daffodils were beginning to fade, but the forest was just starting to green up. I headed behind the building down into the wash and admired the ruby-pink blossoms on the maples as I studied the shrubs with their tiny green leaves that were just starting to unfurl. Below, the sycamores by the stream had just put on enough green to look tinted, and the honeysuckle vines were fully leafed out and ready to steal away any light and food they could on the trees and fence posts they climbed.

My stroll took me past an old farmstead that had been reclaimed by woods, and after I'd walked around the ruins of all the outbuildings, I decided it was time to go back and see how the crew was progressing. I made my way back down to the stream and was just beginning to scrabble back up the other side when I caught sight of a figure at the back of the warehouse. At first, I thought it was just a member of the crew, but then I noticed they were trying to look into the back door of the basement.

"Hey," I shouted. "They're about to take that wall down." I could hear the forklift at the side of the building to the left, and I didn't want anyone to get hurt.

The figure spun toward me and then took off at a run. I tried to get up the hill quickly to chase after them, but the leaves were slick under my feet. By the time I crested the hill, they were gone back into the woods.

I jogged around the building and almost ran right into Saul. "There was someone watching," I huffed. "He was headed for the old road."

Saul didn't hesitate. He jumped into his truck and sped off through a narrow opening to the logging road. I stood waiting for a few minutes, but as my adrenaline started to wear off, I leaned against the hood of my car. Finally, I couldn't wait any longer and called Santiago.

"I should have called you sooner," I said when he answered. "I was hoping Saul would catch him."

"Would catch who, Paisley?"

"The man who was looking into the basement of the warehouse." I sagged down to the bumper. "I was worried he'd get hurt, and—"

"Where are you now?" His voice was alarmed.

"At the warehouse. Saul's crew is here. I'm fine. But Saul

went after the guy on the logging road." Hearing the worry in Santiago's voice made me worried for Saul.

In the background on Santiago's end, I heard a car door slam. "We're on our way. Stay put. If Saul comes back, tell him to do the same." The engine started, and he said, "I'm sending Winslow to you. I'm going after Saul."

"Okay," I said, and I knew I would do what he said. But every part of me wanted to get in my car and go after Saul myself. I stayed put, though, and suggested to the guys that they halt work for a bit. I explained what had just happened, and they immediately parked their trucks and stood around near me. One man even handed me a bottle of water. I was a little uneasy for the moment, but I was glad they were there. When I heard a siren flying down the road, I let out a breath I didn't know I hadn't released. Help was here.

Savannah spun into the parking lot like she was taking a turn in a NASCAR race, and before her car even slid to a stop beside me, she was out and running my way. "Show me where you saw him," she ordered.

I charged around the building, not sure what good it would do to show her but knowing that I just needed to do as I was told. We stopped short by the door, and when I looked down, I saw a small photo of Celeste lying on the ground. Just inside the door, Savannah picked up a white candle. That creep was going to light another candle for her, even as the building came down around him.

A few of the crew members came around the building, and when I pointed to the photo and the candle, they huddled up. Before I knew it, they had stationed themselves at each door and side of the building so that they could keep an eye out for the man who did this if he came back.

"Okay, tell me what you saw," Savannah said as she took out her notebook.

I described the person's height and build, described how they'd been looking in, and then told her that there was something about their gait that made me think they were a man. "I could be wrong about that, though."

"That's good, Paisley. Thanks." She looked at the two guys standing nearby and said, "One of you come with me and one of you stay with Paisley."

"I'm okay. I'll just go sit in my car." I didn't feel unsafe, and I felt awkward with a bodyguard.

"I know you are, and so am I. But none of us should be alone right now." She and the forklift operator began walking in Saul's tire tracks.

The man guarding me smiled, shrugged, and said, "I have soda in my truck. Want one?"

"Bless you," I said as I followed him around front, leaving two crew members to watch the back of the building and each other. We found the remaining three guys out front, all together but facing different directions. No one was sneaking up here again, not if they wanted to remain free to move their limbs.

When my guard opened the cooler in his cab and handed me a cold Cheerwine, I had to resist the urge to hug him. Given his griminess and my shaky emotional equilibrium at the moment, I thought it best to simply sit down in the passenger seat of my car with the door open and flip through my phone some more. My guard obviously felt the same, and so we passed a companionable fifteen minutes of scrolling while we waited.

Finally, Santiago and Saul pulled back around the building, and I relaxed against my seat with relief. But the two men looked anything but relieved. They looked downright angry.

I stood up and walked over. "Didn't catch him."

"Nope, not even close," Saul said. "That car was fast."

"You started a car chase?" I said as I looked at Santiago.

He shook his head. "He did, and I joined in because apparently, I think rural Virginia is Los Angeles." He threw his head back and sighed. "And still we didn't catch him."

I kicked my feet in the gravel. "You tried, though." I wanted to sound encouraging, but my disappointment rang through my words. "It was a man, though?" I asked.

Savannah walked up to join us. "Men's shoes, size nine. So, at least a person wearing men's shoes."

Santiago nodded. "Saul, did you see the person at all?"

"Nope, just a form as he jumped in the car. My impression was of a man, though." He shook his head, "But I wouldn't swear to that."

We stood around in silence for a few moments. I think everyone was just exhausted and sad – at least I was. Eventually, though, Saul said, "Any reason we can't finish the job? I'd like to get it done, and I know Robard will be especially eager to have us take that basement out of here."

Santiago looked at Savannah, who said, "I didn't see anything down there but these two things." She held up the photo and candle she'd placed in an evidence bag. "There could be fingerprints, but I doubt it. Maybe we can take one more look and then . . ."

"Sounds good. Paisley, can you wait for me one more minute?" Santiago studied my face, and I nodded. I really wanted to just go sit somewhere quiet and rest, but I could wait a bit for that. Besides, if Saul's crew was going to keep working, the least I could do was thank them.

I walked over to where they were still milling as Saul

scouted out their remaining work for the day. "Thank you, guys," I said. "I know you didn't sign up for this kind of stuff. I appreciate everything you've done, so will you come over to my house tomorrow night, let me grill some burgers and hot dogs for you? Just casual, to say thanks." I felt really awkward because I couldn't offer these guys much on my budget. I couldn't even afford to invite their families. But I wanted to do something.

"That sounds great, Ms. Sutton," my guard said. "We get off at five. Okay if we come over right after?"

"Perfect. I'll have the grill going so you can eat and get on home. Looking forward to it," I said as I headed back to the car. I passed Saul on the way, and he gave me a wave before pointing his crew to the next areas of work.

I climbed into the driver's seat of my car to wait for Santiago, and, fortunately, the wait wasn't long because I was really done with this place. Really, really done.

He sat down in the passenger's seat and took my hand. "If I knew how to do a spell or something to keep you from coming across this stuff, I would," he said gently. "Are you okay?"

I smiled thinly and said, "I would take that spell because I'm tired of you having to ask that question, even though I appreciate you asking. Yes, I'm okay. Just exhausted."

He sighed. "I bet. Let me cook us dinner tonight at your place. I can make something for Sawyer and then something comforting for us. How does that sound?"

"Now, I've got you saying that, too?" I asked, thinking about how Sawyer always asked me "how does that sound?" when he proposed a plan for the day. "That sounds great," I said.

"So noodles and nuggets . . . and maybe some pad thai for us?" He raised his eyebrows and waited for my reply.

"That sounds beyond perfect. Just remember, I like the spice and the lime," I said and took a deep breath. "Thanks.

"Don't mention it. And Paisley, we got a description of the car and a partial plate. So it's not all bad news." He leaned over, kissed my cheek, and stepped out of the car.

Not all bad news at all, I thought.

A quick call to Lucille confirmed that Sawyer was napping on a ride with his Boppy, and so I decided to stop at Mika's shop before heading over to pick him up. When I came in, she took one look at me and grabbed my arm to get me to a chair. "Hard morning?" she asked as she handed me a bottle of water. Clearly, I looked like I needed hydration, given how many people were giving me drinks today.

I told her about the events of the morning, and she dropped into the chair next to me. "This guy just doesn't know when to quit?"

"I know. You'd think that big equipment might deter him, but apparently not." I took a long pull from the water bottle. "But they did get a description of the car and some of the license plate number."

Mika brightened. "Well, that's good. Octonia's not that big a place, so hopefully, they can find the guy." As her shop bell ran, she quickly stood up and moved in front of me. "Good afternoon, Mrs. Davenport. Is there something you need before I ask you to leave again?"

I stifled a snicker from behind Mika's legs and looked up to see Mrs. Davenport stepping around my friend like she was a lamppost. "Ms. Sutton, I'm actually here to see you. Stop what you're doing. Stop nosing around. Stop inciting all this nonsense. Just stop."

I stared at Creedence Davenport and suddenly realized who she reminded me of: Veruca Salt from *Willy Wonka and the Chocolate Factory*. If she'd had on a red dress with a white collar, she'd have looked just like the little girl from the movie, all stomping feet and pouting. Mrs. Davenport was just a more cosmopolitan and polished version of that spoiled little girl. The comparison made me smile, and then I was laughing so hard I couldn't stop. I tried to contain myself, to come back with a witty retort, but I could only laugh, especially when it was clear that my laughter was making Mrs. Davenport more and more angry.

"The nerve," she said, which sent me into another fit of giggles. "You'll stop all this foolish troublemaking, Ms. Sutton, if you know what's good for you." She stormed out of the shop, slamming the door against the frame.

Mika looked after her and said, "At least she saved me the trouble of kicking her out again." She checked her door's glass and then shut it quietly. "So what got you laughing?"

I said, "Remember Veruca Salt? The character, not the band?"

Mika's eyes grew wide. "Oh my gracious, that's exactly who she is. Too bad we don't have any squirrels or a garbage chute," she said, and then we both broke into guffaws.

Eventually, our laughter subsided, and I realized I might need to use my time to do just the kind of work that Mrs. Davenport was trying to warn me away from. I thought about doing a newsletter about Celeste but decided there were three problems with that idea. First, I didn't want to appropriate Celeste's story for my own gain; second, my newsletter was about history, not about individuals; and third, I didn't really know enough about Celeste as a living person to write an article. Instead, I decided I'd write about structures featuring recycled windows and dedicate this issue of my newsletter to Celeste instead.

I spent the next couple of hours tucked into the cozy chairs of Mika's shop gathering images of rustic greenhouses and houses made from all recycled materials and incorporating them into my article about the uses of old windows. I hoped the article might pique interest in the abundance of old windows I was about to have for sale. It certainly got me thinking, and I decided that if I had a hard time selling any of them, Sawyer and I were going to make our own greenhouse.

I had just put the final touches on my article when I heard familiar footsteps and looked up to see Sawyer plunging headfirst into my lap. "Mama," he shouted. "I didn't know you was here."

"Well, I didn't know you would be here either, Love Bug." I hugged him close. "What a great surprise." I looked up to see my dad smiling.

"I saw your car on the street when we came by after getting ice cream. Thought I might save you the trip out to get him." Dad tousled Saw's hair. "We had fun."

"You did? What did you do?" I asked.

"Boppy took me to a playground," Sawyer said, "and I swung big high."

"Man, that sounds like fun." I stood up. "Thanks, Dad. Come by for a barbecue tomorrow night about five?"

"I'll let Lucille know." He scooped up Sawyer and gave him a big hug. "See you tomorrow. Bye-bye, Buddy."

"Bye-bye, Boppy," my son said as he wiggled free. "Auntie Mickie, will you play with me?" He was off and around the corner before I could remind him that Mika was working.

"What are we going to play, Saw?" she asked as she led him back my way. She pointed at the chair. "You finish. I'm going to teach Sawyer how to use the cash register."

"You sure about that?" I asked.

"I'll put it in practice mode," she answered.

By the time we got home that night, both Sawyer and I were exhausted. But when he saw Santiago's patrol car in the driveway, he perked up . . . and I let out a long sigh and was glad I had told him where I hid the spare key. Dinner was already underway. I had cancelled the usual potluck dinner plans with Mika because I thought Sawyer and I needed a quiet night, and now I was even more glad I'd made that call.

We ate our meal and talked softly and then enjoyed the last hours of daylight by the playground before Santiago headed out and I tucked Sawyer in for the night. This time, when the temptation to stay in bed hit, I gave in and drifted off to sleep beside my son.

The next morning, I called Dad and asked if he'd mind coming to take Sawyer for a walk while I went to the memorial for Celeste that afternoon. I had already explained death to Sawyer when I talked about my mom, and he often asked about Grandma and where she was. But it felt like he was a little too young to understand a memorial service, and I was more than a little nervous that there might be a ruckus of monumental proportions.

Dad said he and Lucille would both come, and they'd take Saw to the library and then head up to the Parkway for a walk and ice cream. I'd plan to meet them at the Big Meadows Lodge a bit later in the afternoon.

Saw and I spent the morning planting carrot, radish, and spinach seeds, and I was fairly sure we had rows with a nice spatter method for half the seeds throughout the bed. I didn't care. I wanted my son to understand that food required work, and I could not wait to see his face when he got to pull up a carrot that he grew.

We ate an early lunch, and then he made me some food in his kitchen while I put on my black slacks for the second time that week and found a black-and-hot-pink blouse to wear with them. I figured Celeste might just appreciate a pop of color today.

On schedule, Dad and Lucille met us by the library. I kissed Sawyer goodbye as they headed inside, and I drove over to the small cemetery at the edge of town. It was beautifully set with a view of the Blue Ridge off to the west. The graves weren't very old here, just going back to the 1930s when people began to bury their loved ones at places other than the local church or their own backyard. But still, I recognized most of the names as those belonging to old Octonia families. Celeste would be among her people here.

I found the small gathering at the upper edge of the cemetery and smiled when I saw that Trevor had secured his friend a prime spot near an old dogwood overlooking the rest of the graves. It would be a quiet place for her, in whatever sense she was there, and for her friends. A bench sat nearby, and I imagined Trevor spending some time there every once in a while, just to talk to Celeste. I'm not sure why I thought of that – too many TV shows, maybe – but I didn't sit at my mom's grave. Probably because I didn't think of her as there. Still, I decided maybe I needed to visit soon, leave some flowers for her and my grandmother and great-grandmother beside her.

Only a few of us were there, Trevor and Ms. Nicholas,

of course, and I was glad to see Saul had come, too. A couple of people about Trevor's age stood near him, and when they comforted him, I was especially glad they were here. I looked around, hoping to see more people arriving, but I didn't see anyone except Kyle Davenport, who stood a bit away from the gathering. I presumed he was respecting Trevor and not wanting to intrude. I smiled his way, and he smiled back.

From the street, Santiago watched the proceedings and the road. He'd told me he'd be here, but as security more than a mourner, as much as he wished he could just pay his respects. It turned out that Trevor hadn't had to do too much at all to get the right to bury Celeste as she wanted. The funeral home had seen his next of kin certificate and been more than happy to make the arrangements as she had wanted them, and when the Davenports had protested, Santiago said, the funeral director had said that they could take it up in court.

As I stared out over the hills, I hoped they wouldn't do that. I really hoped they wouldn't.

Trevor began the service with a few words about how wonderful Celeste had been as a friend and how he had been so deeply honored when she'd asked him to be her legal next of kin. "It meant she trusted me, and I knew trust was something hard to earn from her," he said. He spoke a bit longer and stressed how grateful he was that now she could be laid to rest here, "as herself," he said.

I looked over at Kyle, and I could see tears on his cheeks. I wanted to invite him over, to put my arm around his shoulders, but it wasn't my place. So I said a quiet prayer for his comfort.

Trevor invited anyone there to speak a few words about Celeste, and the two people with him each talked about how much fun she was, how she could dance for hours and still get up and do her job the next day. One woman even talked about how Celeste had been the only person who could explain to her how to walk in tall heels. "To this day, I remember her lessons about setting down my whole foot, not just my toes, when I wear those shoes." I smiled at that idea and wished Celeste could teach me the same.

After everyone spoke, Trevor handed each of us a small purple candle and asked us to light it and lift up a prayer in our own way for Celeste. He lit his flame first, and then the fire passed around to each of us. I studied my flame and then looked at the mound of red clay over what I assumed was Celeste's casket. I didn't know what to pray, so I just said a quiet thank-you and asked for her peace.

Then, Trevor blew his candle out, and we all did the same. The smoke floated up into the sky, and I hope it carried the love from this place up to Celeste. The group stood quietly for a few moments, and then Saul – never one to linger – moved over, shook Trevor's hand, and gave me a small wave before heading to his truck. I didn't plan to linger either, but I did want to give Trevor something. I went back to my car and got the copies of Celeste's books.

"I thought she'd want you to have these," I said as I handed them to him.

He looked down, smiled, and said, "Thank you."

I gave him a quick hug and headed to my car. I looked for Kyle, but he had slipped away. I had wanted to give him a hug, too, but maybe this was for the best. Perhaps he just needed to grieve in his own way.

A quick peek at my phone as I settled in my car showed me the service had only been about fifteen minutes long. I wasn't due to meet Sawyer, Dad, and Lucille for another two hours, so I decided I'd take a little walk myself. Maybe I'd find them along the fire road.

The drive up to the Blue Ridge Parkway was perfect. I enjoyed watching the signs of spring recede as I climbed in elevation, and as I pulled into the waysides and looked out over the valleys below, I admired the shades of green creeping west and then beginning the ascent up the mountainsides. Soon, the mountains would be as awash in green as they would be in gold and red come fall.

When I got to the lodge, I stepped into the restroom and quickly changed into jeans and my walking shoes. Then, I headed across the road and made my way up the wide fire road. Sawyer and I had come here when he was barely walking, and the wind had been so cold that we'd only stayed for ten minutes. Today, though, the sun was warm and the breeze light.

I started off at a brisk pace, eager to get to the tree line and enjoy the wind in the branches. The crowd was thin since it was a weekday afternoon, and I appreciated the space to walk and think. I saw bluebirds darting at the edge of the woods, and their song followed me for a bit as I entered the more shadowed part of the trail. Soon, though, it was the perfect kind of quiet with only the sway of branches for my ears to capture.

Eventually, I decided to wander off the main road and take one of the side trails so that I could have total solitude for just a little bit. Alone time was such a rarity in my life that when I could get truly alone, I relished the chance.

Here, the trail was thinner, and the understory brushed against the legs of my jeans. As I walked, I wondered if deer used these trails, as we've always used theirs, because they were clearer. Then, it occurred to me that these might be deer trails that we'd just appropriated and wondered again if deer preceded and then followed us even now. It was the perfect kind of wandering consideration that let my thoughts rest as my body worked.

I walked deep into the forest and studied the bark on the trees around me, the way the trunks and then the branches reached for the light. I thought of those photographs that showed how the trees kept just enough space between themselves to allow them all to have sunshine. I wondered what it was like to live in real symbiosis with others that way.

Then, I heard the crack of a branch behind me and turned, thinking of all those movies where just that thing happens and the person who heard the sound sees nothing. Sure enough, I didn't see anything there. I smiled and walked on, but on alert.

I went a few yards further, and this time the sound of leaves underfoot was unmistakable. I turned to look, expecting to see a squirrel or maybe a brave deer. Instead, a human-shaped figure ducked behind a tree. If the person had kept walking, I might not have even paid attention, but hiding? Hiding definitely got my attention.

I began to run, fast but steady. I couldn't afford to all-out sprint, not with the distance I had to go before I would reach the main trail – probably another half mile or so – but I could run fast. I fumbled my phone out of my pocket and wasn't surprised to see I had no signal. It was one of the reasons people liked it up here. Everyone needed to disconnect sometimes. Today, though, all of me was screaming for a connection.

Behind me, I could hear footfalls catching up, and while I really wanted to turn around and look, I knew I couldn't afford the time that would cost me. So I picked up the pace and used what little extra oxygen I had to shout "help" as loudly as I could.

I still couldn't see the opening to the fire road ahead of me, so I doubted anyone could hear. But every few seconds, I shouted anyway. And I ran faster.

Still, the feet behind me were catching up. I prayed for strength and speed, and I burst ahead. But it was too little, and a hand clamped down on my shoulder and threw me off balance. I fell to my knees in the dirt and felt pain shoot up through my hip.

I didn't have time to think about pain now, though, so I flipped over and pushed my feet up and out as hard as I could. The bottoms of my Merrells made contact, and the person went flying. I scrambled to my feet and took off again, but this time, a hand grabbed my ankle and sent me sprawling face-first into the ground.

This time, my attacker didn't hesitate, and I felt weight on my legs as the person sat down on me. For a split second, I almost laughed because sitting on someone is the kind of thing I would do if I needed to hold them still, but the fleeting thought gave way to terror very quickly.

"Paisley, I'm going to let you get up, but please don't run. I just want to talk." I knew that voice, and the sound of it made my blood run cold.

Kyle Davenport stood up and pulled me up to face him. "Kyle?" I said. "You really scared me. Why didn't you say something?" I knew this wasn't a casual visit, but I hoped he would think he could make it seem so.

He shrugged. "You just took off so fast." He smiled, and I felt my heart rate triple.

But I knew I needed to mirror his expectations of his conversation. Clearly, he thought it completely reasonable to chase a woman down an isolated forest path and then tackle her to the ground. "Oh, yeah, sorry, too many horror movies, I guess," I said with what I knew had to be the most fake smile I'd ever used. "What did you want to talk about?"

"I saw you at Celeste's memorial today. It was nice of you to come," he said, and I got the distinct impression he felt like he had invited me. "I wish Mother and Father had been there, but, well, they just don't get it."

I nodded, but I didn't think Kyle and I really understood his parents in the same way. "It would have been nice if they had come, that's true. It was good to see you there, though." I was trying to think of a way to get help. Last I checked, it was about forty-five minutes until I was due to meet Dad, Lucille, and Sawyer, but there's no way they'd think to look for me here when I didn't show. "I looked for you afterward to say hi, but you had already gone."

"I saw you looking around and hoped you were looking for me, but I didn't want to talk with Trevor around. He doesn't know Celeste like I do." He looked up at me from under his lashes. "But I think you do."

I had no idea what that meant, and I didn't think I wanted to know. "She seemed like she was a wonderful person," I said. "Joyful, fun."

Kyle draped his arm around my shoulder, and we started walking. Thankfully, either by intention or lack of direction, he was steering me toward the fire trail ahead. "She was so fun. One time when we were kids, she convinced me that I was adopted. I don't remember how she did it, but for a couple of weeks, she had me believing that Mom and Dad had picked me out special because they wanted another little—" He stopped.

"Were you guys a lot alike?" I said out of actual curiosity and the desire to keep him talking as I slowly but surely picked up our pace toward the hope of more people.

He smiled. "We were. Exactly alike. Mama even dressed us

in matching outfits like we were twins." His face grew dark. "Until Celeste wouldn't do it anymore, said she was a girl." The shadows in the forest seemed to grow darker with his mood.

"That must have been hard for you." I had no idea what that would feel like, and my ability to empathize was being largely overrun by fear. But I'd learned that acknowledging someone's pain was never the wrong thing to do.

"It was, and I was really awful to her for, well, for a long time." He seemed to shake off his funk. "But then, I realized that if I wanted my sibling back, I was going to have to accept who she was." He smiled again.

"Good for you, Kyle," I said. I could see the opening to the fire road ahead, and hikers and parents with strollers were passing at regular intervals. All I had to do was get us there.

"It felt good, you know," he said. "I saw her for who she really was at that dance, got to tell people how great she was. We ended in a good place."

All the feeling drained from my hands. "You ended? What do you mean?" Only a couple hundred more feet until we reached the fire road.

"Of course. I accepted her for who she was, but I couldn't handle her changing anymore. It was better that we just keep things as they were. I think she understood." His voice was upbeat and easygoing.

Only a few dozen yards to the road. "May I ask why the night of the dance?" I had to keep him distracted until I could get someone's attention.

"Oh, well, she was so happy that night. She loved to dance, and she was having such a good time. She'd had a couple of drinks, too." He looked over at me with concern. "Not that she was drunk or anything. Celeste had very good self-control. It just made it a little easier for me to catch her off-guard."

"Oh yeah?" I creaked. Almost there.

He sighed. "It was messier than I thought. I just didn't get the knife quite right the first time, I guess. But she died quickly still."

We were there, and as Kyle turned me away from the lodge, I caught sight of Dad out of the corner of my eye. Lucille and Sawyer were looking at something on the ground just behind him. He looked up and saw me.

I couldn't make any sudden movements. If Kyle had stabbed his own sister, there was no telling what he'd do to me, and I couldn't risk Sawyer coming over by even calling out casually. Instead, I dropped my right hand on the side away from Kyle and spelled out "Help" over and over again in American sign language. My dad didn't know much sign, but he knew the alphabet. I just hoped he could see what I was doing.

Now, though, we were walking away from them, and Kyle was still talking. "I took her home to the pool house at first, just so we could spend a few days together. But then – I won't go into the unpleasant details because I want you to remember Celeste as she was – it was clear she had to move on."

I nodded and kept signing. "So where did you take her next?"

"Celeste always loved nature, so I found a quiet place for her to rest amongst the trees and animals." He smiled. "Then, Mr. Greene closed up shop at the warehouse, and I thought it would be so nice for her to spend the rest of her days there. She loved that building, loved working there, loved living there. It really was the perfect place. Since she'd made me a key so I could let myself in, it was easy enough to get her settled there."

My hand was growing stiff from signing the same four letters, but I didn't dare stop. "You set her in a very nice and quiet location," I said. "I'm sorry I disturbed her."

The grip Kyle had on my shoulder grew a bit tighter. "I know you didn't do it on purpose, Paisley, but yes, that was a bit disappointing. I told Mr. Greene the same thing this morning."

"Um, you what?" I whispered as my throat went dry. "You saw Mr. Greene this morning?"

"I did, and you're going to see him soon, too. He's waiting for us at the car." He tightened his grip even further and pushed me along. "We're going to take a little ride, the three of us, so that we can all say goodbye and join Celeste."

I took a deep gulp of air in an attempt to waylay the panic I was feeling. Up ahead, I could see the more secluded parking lot at the other end of the fire road. There was only one car there, and I felt sure it belonged to Kyle. From this distance, I couldn't tell if Robard was in the car. I prayed he was still alive.

Kyle kept talking, but I couldn't pay attention anymore. Every single ounce of my will was shooting out through my fingers as I prayed my dad would see and understand, and every bit of my thought was going toward what I would do when we reached that car in a few moments. I wondered if I could manage to hit Kyle with the door and get away, but then how could I help Robard?

We were just about to step out of the forest and into the parking lot when someone ran right into the back of me, knocking me to my knees again. Kyle gasped as he fell forward, too, but then Dad was there with a boot on Kyle's back as he pressed him into the ground. "You okay, Paisley-girl?" Dad said.

I sobbed out a yes and stood up. "Where's Sawyer?"

"He and Lucille are in a race back to the Lodge. Sawyer was excited to get to really call for help." Dad stared me down. "He thinks it's a game, Paisley."

Tears poured down my cheeks and I sat down on the gravel.

Kyle looked at me from one eye as his face was pressed down into the dirt. "I thought you understood, Paisley. I thought you understood."

I couldn't control the sobs any longer and I sat and let myself weep as hikers began to gather. I could hear Dad explaining that I had almost been kidnapped to a few people nearby and I was grateful because right now I wanted as many people to stay with us as possible.

I was just starting to pull myself together when I remembered Robard. "Dad, Robard Greene is in Kyle's car."

Dad motioned to two young men nearby, and they came to take over holding Kyle down. People really come together when they got to help stop an attempted murder, I suppose. After Dad fished through Kyle's pockets to find his keys, he went to check Kyle's car.

Meanwhile, a woman took the laces out of her hiking boots and then proceeded to tie Kyle's arms and feet with the acumen of a championship rodeo-er. Even through my adrenalize haze, I was impressed.

A moment later Dad jogged over and said that Robard was unconscious in the trunk. He'd sent someone over to the lodge to call an ambulance. "He's breathing okay but has a nasty goose egg." From the ever-growing crowd, a woman stepped forward, said she was a doctor, and headed over to the car. It seemed we were a full-service spectator group here.

I finally felt well enough to stand and levered myself up to my feet. My knees were killing me and I was going to need a massive glass of water as well as a handful of painkillers very soon. But I was okay, and even my terror was subsiding, which was good because just then a car pulled into the lot and my stepmother and son jumped out. Sawyer ran to me hard and fast and was just about to plow, as usual, into my legs when he stopped short and looked over his shoulder at his grandmother. "Are you okay, Mama?" he said.

I could hear a few coos at Saw's cuteness from the crowd as I stepped forward bent down and said, "I am. But the most important question is, did you win the race to call for help?"

He grinned and said, "Of course."

Chapter Fourteen

Santiago and Savannah arrived at the parking lot shortly after Sawyer and Lucille, and I tried not to think about how fast they had to have been driving to make the twenty-five-minute drive in less than ten. I was profoundly grateful to see them and to see Kyle locked up in the back of Savannah's patrol car.

She began taking witness statements by talking with Dad, and Santiago let me sit on the bumper of his car and listen to Dad's rendition of events.

He said the first thing that tipped him off that something was wrong was that I hadn't immediately shouted or waved when I saw him. But then he really grew worried when he realized I had seen Sawyer but had gone the other way. He didn't know who the man was that I was walking with, and that made him concerned, too.

"But when I saw Paisley signing 'help' over and over, I knew she was in trouble. But I wasn't sure if the guy had a gun or a knife, so I had to improvise." I liked the tiny bit of a blush Dad had to his face as Savannah recorded his statement and the crowd listened. "I just knew I had to save my baby girl," he finished.

The crowd erupted into cheers, and I stood up to hug him. "Thanks for saving me again, Daddy."

"Again?" he asked.

"Remember the infamous steak house incident?"

He laughed. "I didn't even know I knew how to do the Heimlich."

"Well, I was glad you did, and I'm glad you could understand my frantic message." I pulled him close and whispered, "I love you, Daddy."

"I love you, too," he said and turned away before anyone but me could see the tears in his eyes.

***

Robard was up and swearing by the time the ambulance arrived, and when I went over to talk to him, he said that Kyle had intercepted him on the way to Celeste's memorial and said he wanted to talk to him about Celeste. Then Kyle had clocked him on the back of the head. "The next thing I knew, some pretty lady was waking me up and asking me what day it was."

He looked me up and down. "Looks like you had a rough afternoon, too."

I stared at the tears in the knees of my jeans and felt the bruise coming up on my cheek from where I'd fallen. "You could say that," I said with a smile. "I'll check in on you later, okay?"

"Not if I check on you first," he said. The ambulance drove off, and I made my way back to the car.

The crowd dispersed slowly after Savannah got their statements so that by the time a news crew arrived to capture the story, almost no one was there. Fortunately, Savannah had just left to transport Kyle back to the jail, and Santiago and I had climbed into Dad's car with Sawyer – thanks to a bystander who had driven to fetch him from the lodge. The reporter stepped out of the news van with her perfectly coifed hair and immediately groaned. "We missed it," she said to the cameraman.

I almost let her go without a story, but then I realized I did have something to say. I stepped out, and the reporter and the camera swung in unison in my direction. The young woman took my name and then asked if I had seen what happened here that day. I sighed and said, "I was actually the victim."

She tried to rein in her jubilation, but she had a hard time suppressing her smile. "I'm so sorry," she said, and I knew she meant it, sort of.

She asked me what happened, and without naming Kyle, I described the events. When she asked me why I had almost been kidnapped, I said, "Because people were too afraid to let other people be who they are."

The reporter looked confused, so I continued. "Today, I went to a small memorial service for Celeste Davenport. I know the discovery of her body has been in the news, but today, I had the opportunity to honor her as a person, not a victim. Oddly enough, the kidnapping attempt today was about that, too. Rest in peace and power, Celeste."

The reporter smiled, a genuine smile this time, and thanked me. I climbed back into the car and said to Santiago, "Can you take my statement at home? I have a barbecue to put on."

Lucille and Dad drove my car back to my house, and I sat holding Sawyer while Santiago drove dad's car. It was a quiet ride home. Even Sawyer seemed to need the space of silence and companionship in the car.

When we got home, though, I gasped. My yard was festooned with beautiful antique-style lights, and a huge smoker was set up in the side yard by the front porch. Saul was in his element as he grilled and sipped his beer.

Tables had been set up along the front porch, and someone had even brought a wireless speaker that was tuned to a nineties station. My front door was wide open, and as I started to step onto my side porch, Mika came out with an armload of sausages and burgers. "You're home," she said.

Then, she set the food down and hugged me tightly. "If this is too much tonight," she said into my ear, "I will send everyone away right now."

I smiled. "It's actually good. I don't think I can manage to help much, though." My knees were throbbing, and I could barely bend the left one. "I had kind of a hard afternoon." I winked.

"Seriously. Let me get Saul this food, and then I want to hear everything." She kissed my cheek and headed off.

Santiago came over and took my hand. "Saul called when you were talking to the reporter, asked if I thought you were still up to this. I hope it's okay that I said yes. I figured you wouldn't want to disappoint the crew."

I nodded. "You are totally right. But this is a lot of to-do for six guys."

"Oh, I invited their families, too," Saul said as he walked over. "I knew you couldn't swing all that food, but I can. The only condition I have is that you don't tell them I did this, okay?"

"I can't take credit for all this, Saul," I said, feeling suddenly weepy again.

"You don't have to take credit," he said. "Just don't give it to me."

I nodded. "Thanks."

"Anytime. Now, you look like a woman who needs a chair, an ice pack, and a drink." He pointed toward the front of the house.

Mika arrived with a Bold Rock Hard Lemonade and led me to a chair by the firepit, a much deeper, more finished firepit than even the lovely makeshift one Santiago had prepared the other night. "Saul did this, too?"

Mika smiled. "Santiago had mentioned that you were hoping to dig this out a bit, so when Saul asked if I'd help this afternoon, I mentioned it. The excavator is out back on his flatbed."

I laughed. "Of course it is, but don't tell Sawyer about the big machine." I looked around. "Speaking of which?" My son had bolted out of the car like his pants were on fire when he'd seen the lights, but then I'd lost track of him.

"Back there." Mika gestured toward the playground down the hill. "Santiago is pushing him on the swing."

I looked down and saw my two guys – I hadn't ever thought of them that way before, but that's what they were – laughing and playing, and something tense from this afternoon eased away.

Dad and Lucille pulled up then, and Lucille climbed out with a cake carrier in her hand. "How did she do that?" I asked Mika.

"I don't ask questions. I just eat," my best friend said.

Soon, all the crew members and their families were gathered on my lawn with plates of food – Saul's grilled goodies and also salads and chips and tiny chocolate croissants that Lucille had, she said when I questioned her about whether she kept an oven in her car, packed for tonight. "I made a few extra for you and Saw, and I'm glad I did." In her case, *a few extra* meant four dozen.

The night was lovely. The peepers were singing along with the radio, and everyone seemed to have a good time. Sawyer played with the crew members' children until he fell asleep in Lucille's lap and she took him up to bed. I stayed in my chair and let my friends wait on me. I was feeling better, but my whole body ached, and the exhaustion weighing down my limbs felt monumental.

At some point, someone handed me a phone cued to the six o'clock news, and my interview was included in a story about Celeste. Apparently, Trevor had contacted the station and offered any trans teen in the area a copy of Celeste's book. I smiled. That was a beautiful way to spread Celeste's joy, for sure.

The crowd thinned out as children reached bedtimes, and I was glad that I'd been able to speak to each of the guys and meet their families. I knew I was going to be working with Saul's crew a lot, and this gathering felt like a good cementing of our working relationship.

Eventually, my friends, my family, and I were left. After everything was tidied up and the bonfire stoked, we gathered our chairs close, the six of us, and settled into the quiet of a cool night. We talked about everyone's children and Saul's skill with the grill, but then, eventually, we knew we needed to talk about Kyle.

Only Santiago knew what had happened in detail, so I told everyone else the story as quickly and emotionlessly as I could. "Poor guy," I said.

"Poor guy?" Mika snapped. "He was going to kill you and Robard."

"I know," I said. "But he really isn't well. I'm not excusing his actions, but his parents really did a number on him when they didn't accept who his sister really was." The emotional trauma of all these things was vast, and I felt like I might need some counseling to deal with it. I couldn't imagine what it must have been like for Kyle.

"I was thinking about that," Santiago said. "Maybe I have been giving Mrs. Davenport an unfair rap."

Saul sat forward and put his hands out toward the fire. "That woman deserves any criticism she receives, as far as I'm concerned."

Santiago sighed. "Yeah, she needs some work, for sure, but we were wrong about who she was trying to protect."

The truth hit me like a wave. "She knew it was Kyle, and she was trying to keep him safe," I whispered. I hadn't been able to understand how she could deny who her daughter really was, but I did understand, with every cell in my body, the fierceness of a mother's love for her son.

Abruptly, I stood up and said, "I'm really tired. Thank you all for coming." I turned to Santiago. "Do you need anything else from me?"

"No, not a thing. Let me walk you in?" He took my arm, and we walked slowly to the house.

I could hear my friends and parents packing up the last of the food and closing up the house. They were profoundly good people, and I was grateful for them. But just now, I needed to be with my son.

"I'll lock up, okay?" Santiago said as he kissed my cheek.

'

I put my hand on his face and said, "Thank you. I'll call you tomorrow." Then, I went upstairs, climbed into bed without getting out of my clothes, and cried myself to sleep next to Sawyer.

The next morning brought bright sun, and when Sawyer woke up and said, "It's day," I actually smiled. It was day, and Sawyer was here, and we had the whole day ahead of us. As usual, while Sawyer snuggled Beauregard, I checked my phone and saw I had a text.

Cappuccino, chocolate milk, and croissants?

I looked at the clock: seven-fifteen. *Nine a.m.?* I replied.

Perfect.

At 9:03, we walked into the coffee shop, a bit late because Beauregard had first insisted on joining us in the car and then had refused to actually get in. Santiago was sitting at a table by the window, and a mug of chocolate milk and a chocolate croissant were sitting by Sawyer's favorite chair. "Hi, Santi," he said matter-of-factly and then picked up his mug. He was getting pretty good at drinking out of lidless cups, but I was still glad to see Santiago had only filled it half full.

At my chair next to Santiago, there was a *huge* vanilla latte with a smiley face in the foam and my very own, very warm chocolate croissant. "Thank you," I said as I leaned down to kiss his cheek.

"It's the least I could do when you solved my case for me," he said and then studied my face. "Are you okay?"

"There's that question again," I said with a grin. "I am. I'm sore and tired, but also okay. You?"

"Tired, too. Was up a lot of last night with paperwork and listening to Kyle's statement, but he told me the same thing he told you." He shook his head. "Normally, I wouldn't be glad to see the Davenports, but when they and their lawyer marched in first thing this morning, I was glad. They're going to try for an insanity defense, I think."

I sighed. "Sadly, I think that may be warranted."

Santiago nodded and slapped the table. "The good

news is, though" – he reached over and tried unsuccessfully to steal Sawyer's croissant – "that I have the day off. What would you all think of a trip to the beach? I have a friend with a little cottage that we can stay in."

The man had just offered to take my son and me to the beach . . . in front of my son, and then, before I could object about the expense, he had offered a free place to stay. I had no objections left, so I said, "Let's do it!" and grinned at Sawyer.

"Great," Santiago beamed as he pulled three to-go cups and a paper cup out from under the table. "Let's get moving."

I smiled and laughed as he transferred our drinks and packed our croissants and then led me to the car. "I don't have clothes or pajamas for us, so we need to swing by the house," I said.

"Nope." He opened the trunk of his car, and there was my suitcase, all packed. "Mika helped me out."

"How did you know I'd say yes? I asked.

"I didn't, but a man can hope." He kissed me quickly and then scooped Sawyer up. "You ready, Little Man?"

My son climbed up into his seat and laughed. "I'm going to throw sand on you."

I groaned. We were going to have to work on beach etiquette during the ride, but that was just fine with me.

Counted Corpse: Chapter One

I tucked my crowbar under the wood and began the dance of prying it off without breaking it. As I worked, I let my mind play back through my memories.

I practically grew up in the manse, the pastor's house, at the church my parents' attended when I was a kid. The pastor's daughter, Sue Ellen, was my best friend, and since my mom was the church music director and the manse was next door, I was there on the church grounds most days.

Sue Ellen was a bit more of a girly girl than I was, or at least her mama thought her one, so she had all these creepy, pristine porcelain dolls that sat on high shelves in her third-floor bedroom. Their frilly dresses and lace caps always puzzled me because it made no sense to me to have toys that you couldn't play with, but Sue Ellen knew better. She knew that some of her role as the pastor's kid was to be a show piece, just like those dolls. That's why she stifled most of her screams when her mother dragged a stiff brush through her, curly, coarse blonde hair on Sunday mornings so that it would look perfect in braids.

I never had that pressure to look perfect, maybe *act* perfect, but never look, and today, as I tightened the bandana over my hair and prepared to pull down the crown molding in this other pastor's house near Bethel Church, I was grateful. My job as an architectural salvager didn't leave much space for primping.

This job had been a long time coming. The deacons at the church had asked me to come in and salvage some key pieces that they wanted to put into their new church addition, and if I would, they were happy to give me anything else I wanted from the hundred-year-old house. They wanted the simple chandelier from the front foyer, the mantel from the parlor, and a lovely old door that led to the dirt-floored basement. Everything else was mine, and I was determined to make the most of this gift.

I'd already hauled out the door and chandelier, and I was just waiting for help from my friend Saul's crew to get out the heavy wooden mantel. Meanwhile, I was doing what I could on my own and popping off as much of the simple but lovely woodwork as I could without damaging it. This molding and the baseboards would be lovely in a farmhouse, and what wasn't salvageable for architecture, Dad would use to make vintage picture frames that I could sell at my soon-to-open salvage store, Paisley's Architectural Salvage.

Architectural salvage had been my career since I had my son and my marriage fell apart more than a year ago. It was flexible in hours, made use of my background in history, and let me feed my desire to go into old buildings without putting me in danger of breaking the law.

This latest job was special because I was, as of two weeks ago, the only white member of Bethel Church, a historically black congregation, and I was eager to do a good job for my new church family, especially after they'd welcomed me so full-heartedly into their pews and hearts.

"Do you want me to try to get this wainscoting down?" My friend and fellow Bethel member Mary Johnson shouted from around the corner in the dining room. "It's pretty, but do you need it?"

I walked through the cased doorway from the study to the dining room and could almost imagine the large, farm table where the pastor and his family had Sunday lunches with different church members after services each week. Mary was poised with her crowbar ready to pull off the dark walnut veneer, and I smiled at her commitment.

Mary and I had become friends when an earlier salvage job had brought me into her life because of her history with an old store in our county, and since then, we'd just grown closer and closer. Now, since she loved this old house and had spent a lot of time here as a child, I'd asked if I could hire her for the day to help me salvage. She had refused payment, but I had a scheme involving an old Singer sewing machine I'd found a couple jobs back and some vintage quilts I'd bought at a flea market. The gift was waiting on her porch, thanks to the generosity of my dad and step-mom, Lucille, for her to find when she got home.

"Yeah, let's see if we can get the pieces off whole," I said as I joined Mary with my own prybar. "If we can, they'll sell for a pretty penny, or maybe the church would even want them for the new fellowship hall?"

"Now that's an idea," Mary said. "We're already putting the mantel in there, so this would make for that cool, old-study feel, wouldn't it?"

I smiled and gently slipped my bar beneath the chair rail at the top as Mary did the same. She was really a natural at this work, and before long, we had gotten all the rails and baseboards off and were well on our way to salvaging more than half of the wainscotting. It looked like the church would have beautiful walnut walls if they wanted them.

As we were about to tug off the last sheet, Saul called from the front door, "Muscle men reporting for duty."

I laughed at my best friend Mika's uncle and put down my tools to meet him. He was alone in the door, and I said, "Are you the muscle because no offense—"

"Stop right there, young lady. I'll have you know I can still pick you up and throw you over my shoulder like a sack of potatoes if you don't mind yourself." He smiled.

"Right, respect my elders. Got it." I laughed as Saul glared at me. "Thanks for coming. The mantel is this way."

I led him through another cased doorway into the small parlor that sat opposite the study, and he whistled. "What a beauty," he said as he ran his fingers over the fine oak grain in the delicately carved wood. "They went all out on this one."

Mary joined us and said, "They did, but the members did all the work. The church records show that the tree from which this mantel was made was felled from a member's land, and one of the congregation's founding members had become a master carpenter when he was a slave. So he did the carving."

I took a deep breath. "I didn't know that. Wow." I joined Saul in caressing the wood. "Let's take extra care, okay?"

Saul nodded. "If it's alright, I'd like to have the piece professionally cleaned for the church, nothing that will change the finish or take off much of the patina. Just shine it up for the new addition. Would that be alright?"

Mary laughed. Saul was always doing very generous things like this, and we had all learned to give him the joy of accepting them without fuss. "Of course, Saul. Thank you. I'll let the deacon board know."

Two young, muscular men walked in, and I said, "Ah, finally, some muscles."

Saul scowled at me and then smiled. "Gentlemen, take care with this beauty. Paisley, you already detached it?"

"All but this one place. I didn't want it falling over. Just a sec." I slipped my smallest pry bar behind the mantel and gently wiggled the final nail from the plaster. As the mantel began to tip forward, the two men took hold of it and lifted it between them with, it seemed, no strain. The piece must have weighed four-hundred pounds, but the two of them carried it out with less effort than it took me to wield a fifty-pound bag of chicken feed from the farm co-op.

With the mantel loaded and off with the chandelier and door to a professional architectural restorer – Saul insisted on having everything cleaned – Mary and I finished up the wainscotting, loaded the used moving truck that I had bought at auction for hauling my goods, and decided to do a final walk-through of the house.

I'd carefully scoured every room on my past visits, but I had, for reasons involving spiders and damp and too many scary movies, avoided the basement. Mary had assured me there wasn't much down there, but I still felt like I needed to take a look, just to be sure. Now that Mary was with me, it seemed kind of silly that I hadn't done it before, especially since the demolition crew was set to come and clear the ground in three days. Nothing like waiting until the last minute to scour a full thousand square feet of space.

Mary and I went down the creaky wooden staircase and stepped into a slightly musty but otherwise completely pleasant basement. The dirt floor was hard-packed and felt like concrete, and the spiders were really minimal. Mary was right, though, the space was mostly empty. There were a few old wooden shelves that had probably once held jars full of pickles and canned tomatoes, and I made a note to carry those out and clean them up since they'd look great in Mika's yarn shop.

I felt the twinge of heartbreak when Mary cracked open the rounded top of an old steamer trunk and watched it crumble to dust in her hand. The trunk was empty, though, so while it was sad to not have the vessel itself, it didn't hold any secret treasures like rare carnival glass or something.

Otherwise, the space was empty, and I felt a pang of sadness that we hadn't discovered a trove of old family treasures stored below ground. It was just as well though because the damp would, as the trunk revealed, destroy most everything.

We were just about to go back upstairs when Mary said, "Hey Paisley, look at this" and pointed to what appeared to be a half-size door just under the upper part of the staircase. I hadn't even noticed that part of the underside of the stairs was closed off since most of them were open to the air below. But this was clearly a storage room, a sort of closet. I immediately thought of Harry Potter and both hoped and dreaded that we might find a small boy living under there.

But when we opened the door, we didn't find a person. Instead, we found a cedar closet, and it was full of leather-bound books, all tucked neatly into shelves and perfectly preserved. "Wow," I whispered."

"Wow is right," Mary said. "These are amazing." She turned to me. "You want them, right?"

"Well, someone needs to have them, so let's take them out and figure out who should keep them. They might belong to someone in the church." Maybe one of the pastors or a member of one of their families had kept diaries, decade's worth it seemed like. I'd have to look at the church history to see who was here long enough to accrue such a collection of writings. If the church granted permission, this would make a great story for my next newsletter.

As we pulled the books out – about four dozen of them – we saw what had preserved them. Behind each set of books on every shelf were small bundles of white chalk tied with twine. They must have used the chalk to absorb moisture, and between that and the cedar, the books were in great shape. The paper and leather alone was gorgeous, and I knew that whatever was written inside would be priceless, especially to the members of Bethel.

I ran out to the truck and got some of the recycled cardboard boxes I hoarded for situations just like this. We loaded up the books and carted them out. Then, by unspoken mutual agreement, we each took one out and began to read.

My journal started, "May 1908 – Today is sunny, and I should be happy. But I can't help think about what secrets lie buried beneath us, about what we had to hide in order to thrive."

I paused, took a deep breath, and watched Mary. Her eyes were wide, and when she looked at me, I thought she might cry. "Listen," she said and swallowed before she read:

July 1910 – Every day I think of what we have kept buried. Every day, I wonder if I should say something. Every day, I start to tell. But then I can't figure out who to tell because what authority in this town will do anything just with what I say. We are just a bunch of colored folks, the bottom rung of the ladder, and no one but us cares about us. The problem is we have to care about the secrets we keep and the people we keep them about, too, and we don't know how to do that, not in this world, not in the way it is now.

Mary and I sat quietly for a few minutes on the truck's bumper. I stared at the open journal in my hands and then looked back at the three full boxes of books behind us in the truck. "I guess I know what we're doing for the rest of the day," I said.

She nodded and closed the book in her hands. "I don't think it's wrong to say that we need to know more before we tell anyone, is it?"

I shook my head. "No, right now what we know is that we found a bunch of journals and that the person writing them is struggling with something. That's not enough to really share, though."

"And we don't even know if this is really fact, right? She – you think it's a she, right?" I nodded – "might be writing a novel or something. Maybe she's inspired by Daphne du Maurier."

I smiled. "Or Henry James. Is it a ghost or not?"

Mary laughed. "Oh, the turn of the screw grows ever tighter." She put her journal back in the box. "Let's get to your place and get reading."

I followed suit, and after we secured the door, locked the house back up, and texted Saul to say we were headed to his lot to unload, we climbed into the cab and drove silently to my new workspace, where we'd left our cars that morning. Fortunately, my son, Sawyer, was with his dad this weekend, so Mary and I could spend the rest of the weekend reading the journals. So by Monday, we could have a plan for what to do and who to tell what.

But first, we needed lunch . . . and reinforcements.

Counted Corpse: Chapter Two

When I texted Mika to tell her what we'd found, she offered to have Mrs. Stephenson, her clerk, watch the store so she could come right over. I was grateful because if we needed to stop the demolition of the house, we only had three days — less than three days — to do it. And something told me we would probably need to stop the demolition.

Neither Mary nor I was willing to do that based on a couple of paragraphs of cryptic journals, though. The church had invested a lot of time and money in architectural renderings and site plans for the new addition, and we weren't going to mess that up for just a hint of a reason. For five years, the members had been donating extra money to add on new Sunday School rooms and a Fellowship Hall that would allow them to turn the basement room they'd used for gatherings into a Youth Center. The new kitchen and ADA-accessible bathrooms in the addition would also mean the church could have more weddings and really serve families for funerals. Nope, we had to be sure something merited a pause if we were going to suggest that.

After unloading everything into my space at Saul's construction lot, we shifted the books into my Subaru and then caravanned the few miles east to my farmhouse. The chickens were wandering far and wide in their hunt for the late summer bugs, and I threw them a handful of cracked corn from the lidded steel container I kept by the kitchen door. My small attempts to keep them tame and near home were working, and Sawyer loved picking up our girls and snuggling them close, even after their latest dust bath.

Inside, we put the boxes on the antique trunk I used as a coffee table and set to a crucial piece of business: what we were going to eat. I wasn't what you'd call a foodie, but after recently switching Sawyer and myself to a mainly vege-tarian diet to benefit our health and help our food choices align with ones that were good for our earth, I had gotten much pickier about what I'd eat. Mary didn't mind that because she was, herself, a true to the bone foodie and an amazing cook, but Mika had a deep affection for sugar and found my decision to eschew bacon a little disturbing.

Still, we were fortunate to live within delivery distance of a couple of great restaurants that served a variety of food, including amazing black bean burgers, so Mary and I decided to splurge and have food brought in. Business had been pretty good for me of late, and now that I was actually able to contribute to Sawyer's college savings fund, I could stand to go wild by ordering a good meal once in a while.

Our order placed and Mika on her way, Mary and I set up a work station. She began by pulling a small card table out from the storage building behind my house, and I grabbed the TV tray tables from my closet. Then, we arranged space to spread out and put notebooks and pens on each small table so we could make notes of names and dates as needed. I'd been a historian long enough to know that documenting what we found was crucial if we needed to go back in and find the information again.

I put out a big pitcher of sweet tea and a bag of dark chocolate candy and confirmed that there was plenty of local hard cider in the fridge. It was going to be a long afternoon, and why not enjoy it.

When Mika arrived, we spent a few minutes sorting the journals by start date and then dividing them into three piles before we sat down to enjoy our meal and talk through our plan.

After Mary and I caught Mika up on where we'd found the journals and the little bit we'd read so far, I shared what had been nagging at me since I'd read the first words in that 1908 journal. "Do you think she means *literally* buried, or is she talking about some sort of cover-up?"

Mary nodded. "I was wondering the same thing, and my sense – for what it's worth – is that she's talking literally."

Mika shivered. "Well, that's not creepy at all," she whispered as she rubbed her hands over her arms.

"Yeah, that's my sense, too." I gathered our empty plates as Mika took the trash to the can. "Guess we need to find out."

Beverages ready but at a distance from the precious journals, we dove in. I had taken the earliest set of journals since that's what I'd started reading before. My books dated from 1908 to 1914. Mika had the next span – 1915 to 1921, and Mary took the final set – 1922 through 1928. We had twenty-one volumes between us, seven each, and I figured if we read until we couldn't any longer, we just might make it through the books by tomorrow evening. I had chosen both sweet tea and cider to fuel my endeavor, and I wasn't surprised to see my two best friends had done the same. It was going to be a long day.

I picked up where I left off after making a few notes about what I needed to know: who was the writer, where was she based, and what was this secret she was talking about. It didn't take me long to figure out the second answer. The third entry in the journal before me read:

When we moved into the manse here next to Bethel, a church member told us what we had to keep to ourselves about our home, and now that secret haunts me. I feel guilty every morning when I wake, and so I spend time here, in the basement, to attend to the truth, to be close and aware, and to record my frustrations in the hopes that someone will remember, some day.

I read that passage aloud to Mika and Mary, and they both gasped. "So she was in the parish house," Mika said.

"And if she's going to the basement . . ." Mary's voice trailed off.

"It sure sounds like she's talking about something literally buried below," I finished as I felt the weight of what we might be discovering settle more firmly on my shoulders. This could be a terrible, terrible discovery.

But if I'd learned anything about investigating something hard from my boyfriend and our county sheriff, Santiago Shifflett, it was best to hold back judgment until we had all the facts. So I went back to reading, as did Mika and Mary.

From time to time, we each read passages out loud, and as we went, I made lots of notes. The author was definitely the pastor's wife, and Mary pulled up the church history on her phone and confirmed that during those years, the pastor had been Rev. Fountain Greene, the founding and longest-standing pastor at Bethel. His wife was named Earnestine, and best we could tell from the contextual clues, she was the author of these journals.

She and her husband had moved into the house in May of 1908, right about the time she'd started writing, and her husband had retired as pastor in 1928, just before the Great Depression descended. So Earnestine's journals spanned her entire time living in the house.

The author and her tie to the manse clear, we plummeted deep to see what we could find about this secret to which she kept referring. References to it were prolific in the first two journal volumes, but as time passed, Earnestine seemed to make peace – or maybe stop thinking about – whatever had bothered her so much when she moved into the house. Over time, she talked more about the people in the community, births and deaths, marriage troubles and children with difficulties. Everything she wrote was compassionate if sometimes very honest, and the more I read, the more I found myself really liking this woman who told it like it was but didn't judge people for their poor choices or past pains.

When dinner time rolled around, I boiled water for pasta, spiced up the jarred spaghetti sauce, and made my quick and easy broiler garlic bread with lots of butter and slices of fresh garlic. Then, I ran out to the garden, harvested the first of the spinach and the lettuce that had managed to survive a Virginia summer without bolting thanks to a shady garden spot, and mixed up a quick green salad. Then, I called my friends to the table for a break, a bottle of wine, and some sustenance. It didn't look like any of us were ready to quit, and with only one or two more journals apiece left to do, we might just be able to finish reading tonight.

Mika helped me set the table, but Mary was absolutely engrossed in whatever she was reading. When she didn't join us after a few minutes, Mika and I picked up all three wine glasses and went back in the living room. The food could wait, and it looked like Beauregard, my gray Maine Coon Cat, was content to sleep with his head on Mary's knee as she continued to read, so our food wasn't in danger from his sometimes pesky paws.

For a few minutes, Mika and I sipped and watched Mary read, glancing at each other with raised eyebrows more than once. Clearly, Mary was intent on finishing, and neither of us dared interrupt.

Finally, just as I was about to get up to pour more wine, Mary closed the journal she was reading, sat back, and said, "Well, we definitely need to adjust our plans for the addition."

I studied her face for a minute and formulated about a million questions, but she still seemed to be considering, weighing what she learned, and I knew she'd share when she had a grasp on what Earnestine's words had revealed. So I sipped what was left in my glass, decided that any more reading I would need to do would have to wait until tomorrow, and felt a bit of pressure ease off. It seemed we had the basic information we needed, if what Mary had learned was as weighty as it seemed, so we could discuss and process a bit before finishing our reading.

After a few more minutes of quiet, Mary said, "There's a Monacan burial mound underneath the manse."

I felt my mouth drop open and stared, unblinking, at my friend as I waited for her to say more.

Mary held up the journal. "In 1928, Earnestine couldn't keep the secret any longer and wrote down all she knew in these pages. Then, she brought up what she knew to the deacons of the church and threatened to go to the newspaper."

"How did the deacons react?" Mika asked in an awed whisper.

"I don't know. Her last entry was written just before she went to the meeting." Mary's face was strained and her jaw tight.

"What?!" I shouted.

Mary sighed. "There's nothing more. That's the last entry." She opened the journal and held it up. As she flipped the pages, I saw no words, only blank paper. She hadn't finished the journal.

"Someone killed her," Mika said.

I turned to look at my friend and shook my head. "We don't know that."

"Well, why else would she stop when she'd kept a journal for twenty-one years?" Mika asked. "What other reason could there be?"

I shook my head again. "I don't know, but we can't jump to conclusions." Dinner forgotten, I grabbed my laptop and opened a genealogy site. I put in the name Earnestine Greene in Octonia, Octonia County, Virginia, and hit search.

It only took a second for the results to return, and I immediately clicked on her death certificate. I scanned the date – August 8, 1928 and looked at Mary. "What's the date of that entry?" I whispered.

Mary flipped back two pages. "August 8, 1928."

I yelped involuntarily and then spun the screen so my friends could see. "She died that day." Both Mika and Mary groaned as I turned the laptop back to me. "It says the cause of death was head trauma, likely from a fall down the stairs." I swallowed the baseball in my throat.

"I think that's pretty clear," Mary said, "but not proof. She could have been so upset that she tripped and fell. Or just missed a step. I've done that."

I sighed. "Yes, that's true. But either way, I think we need to call Santiago. Something horrible happened, and we need him to investigate."

As I told my phone to call my boyfriend, my friends moved the journals back to the boxes, leaving the three that Mika and I still hadn't read out on the table. Then, Mika fixed us each a plate, put all of them on warm in the oven, and finally got out the other bottle of wine. We were going to need it.

Grab your copy…
vinci-books.com/counted

About the Author

ACF Bookens lives at the edge of Virginia's Blue Ridge Mountains with her young son and three playful cats. When she's not writing, she cross-stitches, plays too much Roblox with her kid, and does historical research on enslaved communities in the area.